# THE BARBARA CARTLAND ETERNAL COLLECTION

The Barbara Cartland Eternal Collection is the unique opportunity to collect all five hundred of the timeless beautiful romantic novels written by the world's most celebrated and enduring romantic author.

Named the Eternal Collection because Barbara's inspiring stories of pure love, just the same as love itself, the books will be published on the internet at the rate of four titles per month until all five hundred are available.

The Eternal Collection, classic pure romance available worldwide for all time .

I0607963

# THE LATE DAME BARBARA CARTLAND

Barbara Cartland, who sadly died in May 2000 at the grand age of ninety eight, remains one of the world's most famous romantic novelists. With worldwide sales of over one billion, her outstanding 723 books have been translated into thirty six different languages, to be enjoyed by readers of romance globally.

Writing her first book 'Jigsaw' at the age of 21, Barbara became an immediate bestseller. Building upon this initial success, she wrote continuously throughout her life, producing bestsellers for an astonishing 76 years. In addition to Barbara Cartland's legion of fans in the UK and across Europe, her books have always been immensely popular in the USA. In 1976 she achieved the unprecedented feat of having books at numbers 1 & 2 in the prestigious B. Dalton Bookseller bestsellers list.

Although she is often referred to as the 'Queen of Romance', Barbara Cartland also wrote several historical biographies, six autobiographies and numerous theatrical plays as well as books on life, love, health and cookery. Becoming one of Britain's most popular media personalities and dressed in her trademark pink, Barbara spoke on radio and television about social and political issues, as well as making many public appearances.

In 1991 she became a Dame of the Order of the British Empire for her contribution to literature and her work for humanitarian and charitable causes.

Known for her glamour, style, and vitality Barbara Cartland became a legend in her own lifetime. Best remembered for her wonderful romantic novels and loved by millions of readers worldwide, her books remain treasured for their heroic heroes, plucky heroines and traditional values. But above all, it was Barbara Cartland's overriding belief in the positive power of love to help, heal and improve the quality of life for everyone that made her truly unique.

# AUTHOR'S NOTE

In January 1906 Frank Marriott's streamlined Stanley Steam car recorded 127.66 m.p.h. on Daytona Beach. In the same year at the Olympia Motor Show Rolls-Royce presented a new six cylinder 40/50 car that was to win everlasting fame as the Silver Ghost.

Henry Ford's amazing Model T, produced in 1908, sold fifteen million cars before it was dropped in 1927.

The race in 1908 from New York to Paris was won by Roberts and Schuster in a six cylinder American car, the Thomas Flyer. They took one hundred and seventy days.

# CHAPTER ONE
## 1907

Susanna walked down the back stairs and, moving along the passage, entered a sitting room that was seldom used.

This was her way of approaching the drawing room, for she knew that if she went down the front stairs Hibbert, the butler, would insist on announcing her.

If there was one thing that made Susanna really shy it was to walk into the drawing room where all her mother's friends were gossiping round the tea table.

At the sound of her name there would be a silence and all eyes would be turned towards her as she advanced into the room.

She knew only too well how unprepossessing she looked, far too fat and ungainly even in her new gown, lacking the small and elegant waist that was part of the beauty that made her mother acclaimed wherever she went.

Lady Lavenham was one of the famous beauties who made people stand on their seats in Hyde Park to watch her and who was described in every newspaper as one of the most beautiful women in England.

What they really meant was that she was one of the most beautiful women in the King's circle and therefore envied by everyone else in Society.

Susanna knew that it was a cross for her to bear that her second daughter was not beautiful but decidedly plain.

Susanna would stare at her reflection in the mirror and wonder what she could do about her round, puffy pudding face in which her eyes, nose and mouth seemed much too small.

Her hair too, instead of being the shining gold of her mother's or the attractive darkness of her father's, was an unimpressive compromise between the two.

When she had looked at herself for some time, she would invariably go to the drawer where she kept a box of chocolates and nibble away until the cloying sweetness of them made her feel slightly better.

It was only by eating that she could somehow recompense herself for her mother's sharpness and her father's disappointment.

Her sister May had been so different. She had been slim and lovely long before she emerged from the schoolroom as a *debutante*.

"May is as beautiful as you were when I first met you," her father would often say and only Susanna was aware that it brought a little frown to her mother's white brow because she disliked rivals of any sort even if it was her own daughter.

But one thing was quite obvious that there was no thought of any rivalry where Susanna was concerned.

As she crossed the sitting room now and entered the writing room that adjoined the drawing room, she could see a reflection of herself in several gilt-framed mirrors and realised that she looked dumpy.

That was exactly the right word!

'Rather,' she told herself with a flash of humour, 'like a cottage loaf!'

Her waist was pulled in tightly to try to make it seem smaller, so that her body bulged above and below it.

The dress she was wearing, of oyster crêpe trimmed with pleated frills of silk round the hem, would have made May look like a young Goddess, but on Susanna it merely appeared dowdy.

'There is nothing I can do about it,' she told herself defiantly.

She felt a sudden longing for the small meringues and little pink-iced cakes that she knew would be part of the elaborate tea in the drawing room and she quickly crossed the room to the communicating door.

As she turned the handle very softly, she heard her name mentioned.

"At which Reception are you presenting Susanna?" a voice enquired.

"Oh, the first," her mother replied. "It's a tiresome bore, so the sooner I get it over with the better."

"After that what plans have you made for her, Daisy?" someone else asked.

Lady Lavenham laughed, a tinkling laugh that her admirers described as sheer music.

"Marriage, of course," she replied, "and quickly!"

"You are quite right," the first speaker approved, whose voice Susanna recognised as that of Lady Walsingham, "and who have you in mind for her? Another Duke?"

There was a little burst of laughter at this, before Lady Lavenham responded coolly,

"But of course."

Susanna realised that, holding onto the ornate doorknob, her fingers were stiff.

Lady Walsingham now asked,

"Which Duke? Do tell us, Daisy, who you have in mind."

"And I hope you will all help me," Lady Lavenham replied, "I will be frank and tell you that the only Duke who is eligible at the moment is Southampton."

There was a little shriek following the almost breathless hush as Lady Lavenham spoke and then Lady Walsingham said,

"But my dear Daisy, Hugh Southampton has not a penny to his name!"

"Exactly!" Lady Lavenham replied. "That is why he will be delighted to marry Susanna."

There was another hush before someone enquired tentatively,

"Are you telling us that Susanna has money?"

"Of course she has, " Lady Lavenham replied. "I thought you knew that her Godmother, a most tiresome woman, left her a fortune."

"How exciting! I had no idea," Lady Walsingham exclaimed and the other ladies round the tea table joined in with cries of astonishment.

"Poor Susanna will need every penny of it," Lady Lavenham went on. "We all know that Hugh Southampton needs a rich wife, so what could be more convenient?"

"What indeed?" someone added. "Really, Daisy, you are a genius. But then you always have been."

There was a note of envy in the speaker's voice because Lady Lavenham's elevated position in the Social world had inevitably made her a number of bitter enemies.

"It's not fair," they had often complained, "that she is not only beautiful and has married the charming Charles Lavenham, who, being such a good shot, is *persona grata* in the sporting world, but she is also amusing enough to captivate the King and to have married her first daughter, May, to the Marquis of Fladbury, who on his father's death will be the Duke of Haven."

But dear Daisy's second daughter was undoubtedly so fat and plain that she would be a brake on the meteoric ascent of her mother to the social pinnacle that no one could depose her from it.

To have learnt now that the ugly duckling was an heiress was too much!

Most of the ladies were thinking privately that the Duke of Southampton, whose ancestral home was crumbling around his ears and who owed money in every direction, would be only too delighted to sell his title for a wife who was rich and English.

He had, as they well knew, been taking a critical look at some of the American heiresses crossing the Atlantic in the hope of acquiring a distinguished husband.

The only ones who were even passably tolerable had preferred more important Dukes or rather their mothers had preferred them.

It was understood in the strange unwritten code of Edwardian Society that a mother's job was to marry off her daughter as soon as she left the schoolroom into the highest Society position obtainable.

What the daughter felt was of no consequence whatsoever.

Susanna, listening at the door, could hear her sister May repeating over and over again,

"I cannot marry him, Susanna, *I cannot*! I hate him and when he touches me I feel sick inside."

Susanna remembered May sobbing her heart out night after night.

No one, except herself, would listen to what she said and dressed as a bridesmaid Susanna had followed her up the aisle of St. George's Church, Hanover Square, and heard her take her marriage vows in a weak tearful voice.

She too had disliked her brother-in-law from the moment she had seen him. However red-faced he was from the quantities of claret he consumed, he was acclaimed by everyone, including her father, as a fine sportsman and a first class shot, and no one would have found it credible that May might have other ideas for a husband or find the Marquis repulsive.

When May had come back from her honeymoon, white-faced and dull-eyed, she was, for the first time in her life, uncommunicative with her younger sister.

Susanna had told herself then that never, never would she be forced into matrimony with any man. But she knew now, as she listened to what was being said, that it was not going to be easy.

Lady Lavenham ruled her husband and her children with a rod of iron. As it happened she had had very little interest in her daughters, finding them boring when they were small and gauche and tiresome when they were older.

She was pleased, when following two unwanted daughters she was able to present her husband with a son and heir. But that, she said firmly, was the end of the family.

Henry was now at Eton, a handsome little boy remarkably like his father, and in the holidays his mother, as a special favour, often took him driving with her in Rotten Row.

It was a treat that occasionally she had accorded to May, but it was something that had never happened to Susanna.

She was well aware that it was because her mother thought her plain and unattractive and would never admit that anything connected with herself should be anything but perfect.

This meant that she was ashamed of her second child and Susanna therefore was kept more in the background even than May had been.

Children were expected not to be either seen or heard.

When they were small, at five o'clock they were brought downstairs by Nanny and taken into the drawing room for exactly half an hour.

Their mother's guests enthused over them and they would be given a sweet biscuit. Then they were supposed to sit quietly in a corner until Nanny collected them and took them upstairs to the nursery.

It was an ordeal that had made Susanna embarrassed even when she was very small and it was an inexpressible relief when, as she grew fat and plain, her mother said two girls in the drawing room were too many and May was to come down alone.

"It's not fair," May would protest furiously upstairs when Nanny made her change into one of her best dresses, "that I go downstairs and Susanna stays up here."

"You know the answer to that," Nanny would reply sharply. "You obey your mother and make her pleased with you, otherwise you'll be sorry."

"I will not be sorry, I should be glad if she does not want me," May retorted, but she had been taken down regardless.

Susanna had been quite content to stay behind in the nursery.

It had been the same when they were at Lavenham Park in Hampshire.

When they were in the country, they were much happier being free from the constraints that were inevitable in London.

They could ride their ponies, play hide-and-seek in the shrubberies, steal peaches from the kitchen garden and be hardly aware of the large house parties their mother gave, except sometimes they would peep over the banisters when the King had arrived.

Once there had been three Kings staying in the house at the same time and, despite the fact that they felt it was patriotic to admire King Edward, it was inevitable that they should find the dark handsome King Alphonso of Spain the most attractive.

But it was impossible for the children, although far away in the nurseries on the third floor of the West wing, not to realise what a commotion there was when the King was a private guest.

Supplies of his favourite aubergines, ginger biscuits from Biarritz, bath salts and cigars were all ordered in abundance.

One room in the house would have to be converted into a private postal and telegraph office. And at Lavenham Park the lines had to be brought ten miles cross-country.

The King's entourage included equerries, valets, his secretary and grooms and in the shooting season, loaders, horses and dogs as well.

Whether there were three Kings or not staying at Lavenham Park, Susanna when she watched her mother's guests going down to dinner thought that it always appeared to be a Royal procession.

Her mother with her tiny waist and her tulle-encircled shoulders would be ablaze with diamonds from a huge tiara on her carefully waved hair to the sparkling diamond buckles on her satin evening shoes.

The ladies who followed her were just as magnificent if not so beautiful.

As it was inevitable that every gentleman who stayed with them should bring a valet, so every lady brought a lady's maid carrying in her hand a large leather jewel case emblazoned with its owner's coronet.

When King Edward VII was staying in the house, the diamonds, the tiaras, necklaces, brooches, earrings and bracelets seemed to encase every lady guest almost like a coat of mail.

Everyone in the household, even in the nursery, knew that the King expected women to glitter and his sharp reprimand when the Duchess of Marlborough had appeared at dinner wearing a diamond crescent instead of the expected tiara lost nothing in the telling.

Susanna had watched May put on the Haven jewels when she came home with her husband soon after she had married.

The tiara of emeralds and diamonds, which seemed almost like a crown, had a necklace to match it and a colossal bow brooch that May pinned in the front of her bodice.

"You look like the Queen of Sheba!" Susanna had exclaimed.

Then she had seen the unhappiness in her sister's eyes and knew that no jewels, however magnificent, could compensate her for what she had to endure from the proximity of the Marquis.

"Are you very – unhappy, May?" she whispered.

May had not looked at her sister, she had only stared in the mirror as if she saw, not the reflection of herself but a picture of the years ahead.

For the moment Susanna thought that she was not going to answer.

Then she said in a voice that was curiously old,

"I cannot talk about it, Susanna. There is nothing to say, nothing I can do, so please don't ask me any questions."

It seemed to Susanna after that, as if May was avoiding her until she had driven away with the Marquis in his smart travelling carriage.

She had kissed Susanna goodbye and her arms had seemed for the moment to cling to her sister as if she could not bear to let her go.

Although neither of them said anything, Susanna knew that it was an agony for May to leave home and drive away with the man she hated but she now belonged to.

'That must never happen to me,' Susanna had thought then.

Now standing at the drawing room door, she felt as if what she was hearing was the strike of doom.

She closed the door very very softly, then turned and walked back the way she had come up the back stairs to her bedroom which adjoined the schoolroom on the third floor.

In London the nursery had been renamed the schoolroom when Nanny left and was replaced by a Governess.

While Nanny had always seemed to be a fixture, Governesses changed frequently, owing to the fact that they disliked Lady Lavenham and she found them incompetent and never restrained herself from saying so.

"I can tell you, my Lady," one of the Governesses had said in Susanna's hearing, "that the Countess of Bressington was very satisfied with me for the ten years I was with her."

She went and so did the two Governesses who followed her. Then, as far as Susanna was concerned, a miracle occurred.

Miss Harding was a teacher, tactful enough to placate Lady Lavenham, who could engage a pupil's interest and stimulate her mind.

May unfortunately had only a year with Miss Harding before she married, but Susanna was taught by her for over two years.

To her Miss Harding had been a revelation because she had not only been able to answer all the questions that had puzzled her but directed her curiosity into the right channels so that she could find the answers for herself.

Lady Lavenham was not in the least interested in her daughters' education, except that they should learn to speak French and Italian fluently.

Lord Lavenham often said that he found it a bore when he was staying at Sandringham to be obliged to converse both in French and English at the same time during a meal, changing from one language to the other, perhaps even in the same sentence.

But it was second nature to Lady Lavenham, who was determined that her daughters should not be deficient in this if in anything else.

Otherwise she was completely indifferent to what else they learnt or did not learn, except that they should be good housekeepers and be able to add up the bills and write a cheque.

This was something she never did herself as she employed an extremely efficient secretary to do it for her, but she told her daughters,

"If you have no wish to be cheated by inefficient servants or crafty ones, then you must understand money."

In this Lady Lavenham was different from many of her contemporaries who merely understood how to spend money and do so with considerable success!

Susanna, however, had rebelled at finding herself restricted to nothing but arithmetic and French and Italian verbs.

She had started by being interested in history, but then she had realised that literature could be enthralling not merely in the novels that were the fashion of the moment or the insipid short stories that appeared in ladies' magazines.

When she was reading, she could forget the disappointment she was to her father and her mother and her own reflection in the mirror.

It was Miss Harding who taught her about art and made her appreciate the pictures that hung on the walls of her home and those that they could admire in the National Gallery.

She had never realised before that her mother knew little of such things and was more concerned with the plants in the conservatory and the hothouse flowers that decorated the drawing room than the family treasures that had been accumulated by the Lavenham ancestors.

To Susanna it was a new world.

She and Miss Harding searched the bookshops for volumes that contained reproductions of pictures to be found in the great Galleries of Europe such as the Louvre in Paris and the Uffizi in Florence.

Every time she found a picture she particularly liked, Susanna began to feel that it was a treasure that belonged to her and that she owned it in a way that was impossible to explain in words.

Then most unexpectedly at the beginning of the year Lady Lavenham had told Miss Harding that she would be expected to leave in three months' time.

Without waiting for an explanation from her Governess, Susanna had rushed downstairs to her mother's boudoir in a manner that she had never done before and burst in on her.

"I hear, Mama, you have given Miss Harding notice!" she cried. "Why? Why must she go? I cannot lose her!"

Lady Lavenham was lying on a *chaise longue* wearing one of the clinging chiffon tea gowns that were the fashion for every lady in the afternoon.

It was a relief, Susanna understood, for the wearer to take off the tightly laced corset that pulled in her waist.

She was too innocent to know that the tea gowns had been invented for a very different reason.

She was, however, aware that when her mother was in London, the King and sometimes other gentlemen would call for an intimate hour when no one under any circumstances was to disturb her.

Fortunately, as they were in the country, Lady Lavenham was alone and the house party was not being expected until the following day.

"Kindly do not burst in on me in that rough manner," Lady Lavenham said in an icy voice that usually made her daughter tremble.

At the moment Susanna was too upset to feel anything but indignation.

"Why have you told Miss Harding to leave, Mama?" she enquired.

"You are being rather more stupid than usual," Lady Lavenham replied. "Your hair is untidy and I can see there is a spot of ink on your dress."

"I asked you a question, Mama!"

"Then I suppose I must explain it in words of one syllable," Lady Lavenham replied, "that as you are over eighteen, in fact almost too old to be a *debutante*, were it not that you were in mourning last Season, you are to be presented."

Susanna looked at her wide-eyed.

"But does that mean Miss Harding must leave?"

"But of course. You would hardly want a Governess when you are 'out' and I presume, boring though it will be, I shall have to chaperone you everywhere."

There was no doubt from the way she spoke that Lady Lavenham would find the task unpleasant.

Then she added sharply before Susanna could speak,

"For Heaven's sake go upstairs and make yourself look more presentable. God knows how I will ever get you off my hands looking as you do now."

For a moment Susanna stood staring at her mother. Then, as the blood rose crimson in her cheeks, she turned and walked from the boudoir.

Upstairs she went into her bedroom and sat on the bed feeling as if unexpectedly her whole world had fallen about her ears.

It was foolish of her but she had forgotten that she would have to make her debut and would be taken, as May had been, from ball to ball and from Reception to Reception. She knew that she would hate every moment of it.

How could she do anything else knowing that her mother was ashamed of her? That no man unless he was forced to do so would dance with her?

Foolishly it had never struck her that because she was to 'come out' she would lose Miss Harding.

She had been happier these last two years than she had been in her whole life, but she knew now that she might have realised that she was living in a fool's paradise because she ought to have made her debut the previous summer.

It had been impossible because her grandmother had died and they had been plunged into deep mourning that made her mother look exquisitely lovely while she herself resembled a fat crow!

But now at eighteen and a half she would emerge on the Social world and she was intelligent enough to realise that from her mother's point of view as well as her own, it would be a disaster.

The idea was so horrifying that Susanna sought for a bag of sweets that she had bought from the village shop and stuffed several of them into her mouth at once.

'I shall look awful and feel worse,' she told herself, 'and when Miss Harding goes there will be no one to talk to and no one to be interested in anything I think or want to discuss.'

Then, as if everything moved with the smoothness of one of the new Express trains, plans were made to open the London house, to leave the country and for Miss Harding to say 'goodbye'.

The night before she left, Susanna had cried until she could cry no more.

"What shall I do without you?" she sobbed. "You are the only person who has ever been kind to me, the only person who has treated me as if I was real. When you are gone, there will be no one!"

"Quite frankly, Susanna," Miss Harding had said in her quiet voice, "there is little more I can teach you."

Susanna had been so surprised she stopped crying and stared at her Governess, the tears wet on her cheeks.

"It is true," Miss Harding said. "You must realise by now that you are very intelligent, far too intelligent for the life you will live."

"But I shall – have to – live it," Susanna answered.

"I suppose you must," Miss Harding said with a sigh, "and there is no alternative for a girl born into your position in life. But it need not stop you from thinking, reading and from developing."

"For what?" Susanna asked bitterly.

"For yourself," Miss Harding replied.

She paused for a moment as if she was choosing her words carefully and then she said,

"Some people are completely happy with the Social round, the excitement of giving a bigger and better dinner party tomorrow than the one they attended yesterday, but I think you are different."

"I hope – so," Susanna murmured.

"I am sure you are," Miss Harding said, "and I therefore think, Susanna, that you will always find new horizons for yourself. If you cannot do actually all you want to do, you can at least, do it in your imagination."

Susanna clasped her hands together.

"But – you will not be here to – help me."

Miss Harding paused a moment before answered,

"I have always believed that when we need something very much, and I am talking spiritually and not materially, someone is there to guide and help us. If it is not a person, it is books, music or prayer, we are never left entirely alone."

Susanna was still for a moment and then she said,

"I understand what you are saying to me, but it will be hard, very hard, and I am not likely to find anyone to help me amongst Mama's friends."

Miss Harding thought the same thing, but she knew that it would be disloyal to say so.

Instead she replied,

"You have to believe in yourself, Susanna. You have to find your own way, choose your own direction and, because I know you so well, I know that eventually you will not fail yourself."

"Or you," Susanna added quietly.

"I shall be thinking of you," Miss Harding said, "and let me tell you, I have never had a pupil whom I have loved more or of whom I have had such high hopes."

Her words brought the tears into Susanna's eyes again, but now they were not tears of despair but of delight because no one had ever given her such words of praise before.

When Miss Harding had left, Susanna had cried again because she could not control her own unhappiness. She felt as if she was starting another life that she knew nothing about.

Lady Lavenham had taken her to London earlier than was normal because Susanna had to be provided with a new wardrobe.

Every morning they drove to the shops and spent what to Susanna seemed long weary hours choosing materials, having fittings, buying shoes, gloves, sunshades, hats and lingerie in a way that made her feel as if she was being fitted out for an expedition that might last for twenty years.

"I must try at least to make you look presentable," her mother had said sharply, when Susanna had suggested that she had too many gowns.

Then she had added,

"Your father has said I can spend as much as I like, so you might as well try and be grateful even though unfortunately we cannot alter your face or your figure!"

Every moment she spent alone with her mother made Susanna feel more insignificant. She could see the difference between them reflected in every shop window.

The intonation in the voices of her mother's friends when they met them in Bond Street or in the shops would have been humorous if it had not been so hurting.

"Daisy, darling!" they exclaimed. "How exquisite you look, like a breath of spring. Oh! Is this Susanna?"

There was always a pause before the last three words. A pause Susanna knew meant that they were surprised and even a little shocked at her appearance.

She knew too that the dressmakers thought dressing her to be a waste of time except that the bills mounted higher and higher in their efforts to try to make her appear attractive.

They laced her into boned corsets until she could hardly breathe. She would try on bodices, embroidered, frilled or ruched, but whatever the trimming the effect was the same, she would merely look fat.

Hairdressers came to the house to try out new arrangements for her hair.

When her mother inspected their efforts, it was obvious that they had effected little difference and they metaphorically shrugged their shoulders as if they longed to be brave enough to say that they had been given hopeless material to work on.

Fittings and more fittings! In and out of shops!

Susanna had done nothing else for the last month, and now it was nearly the end of March and the first drawing room was scheduled to take place at the beginning of April.

She found herself counting the days until the Season would be over and they could return to the country.

There she would be able to ride and she would not have to stand for hours in stuffy dressmakers' shops. She would walk in the garden without being accompanied by either her mother or the housekeeper who escorted her when Lady Lavenham was busy.

She missed Miss Harding almost unbearably.

Because she felt that it would please her Governess, Susanna, whenever she went out with anyone except her mother, always insisted on the way home on stopping at a bookshop.

The pile of books in her bedroom grew every day, but the difficulty was to find time to read them.

Fortunately, until she was presented, she was not allowed to go down to dinner parties and only came downstairs to dinner when her father and mother were alone or joined by relatives.

Then when they gossiped and chattered Susanna tried to understand what they were talking about and attach the scandals that they lowered their voices over, to the right person.

It was like, she thought, listening to a foreign language and only understanding half of what was said.

It seemed too rather like reading a very badly written novel.

The fact that Isobel had lost Henry who had danced attendance on her for over a year might have been more interesting if Susanna had been able to fathom who Isobel and Henry were.

That Bertie had gone big game shooting, because he had come home unexpectedly one day and discovered what he had long suspected, was completely incomprehensible!

'Oh, to be at Lavenham!' she kept saying to herself.

The thought of the sunshine on the lake, the scent of the woods and the blue haze over the hills was like a drop of water to a man in a desert dying of thirst.

Now shatteringly and horrifyingly, she knew that she would not be able to go home. She would be married to the Duke and, just as May had been, exiled from everything that was familiar and everything that had meant, if nothing else, security in her own small world.

'It's impossible! I cannot face it! I will not marry a man who only wants my money,' Susanna told herself.

She had known, although she had almost forgotten, that her Godmother had left her a fortune when she was ten.

"Susanna! Why Susanna?" her mother had asked querulously at the time.

But then as she understood as she grew older that her father handled her money and would do so until she had a husband, it really had seemed of no particular interest.

Lord Lavenham was quite a wealthy man and a generous one. Her mother had everything she wanted and, although the cost of the parties when they entertained at Lavenham Park must have been astronomical, he never complained.

There would often be thirty guests, with sixty visiting servants and their own huge domestic staff in the big Gothic-style house that towers, gargoyles and a great deal of stone masonry had been added to in her grandfather's time.

It was, Susanna knew, in bad taste but it was her home and she loved all of it.

Now, because she had a fortune, she would be a Duchess and would live somewhere else and her mother would be pleased with her for the first time in her life.

Upstairs in the schoolroom, which had always seemed empty now that Miss Harding had gone, Susanna flung herself down in the chair in front of the fire.

All she could see at the moment was May's unhappy face and hear the agony in her voice.

She wondered if she could go to May and ask her advice, but she knew that if May had not been able to prevent her own marriage to a man she disliked utterly, she would be quite unable to do anything about her sister's.

'What can I do?' Susanna asked herself and her thoughts flashed to Miss Harding.

If only she could go to her. If only she could talk to her, she just knew that she would understand.

But Miss Harding had written only two days ago to say that she had found employment with the Duchess of Northumberland and had therefore gone North.

'I have to think,' Susanna told herself. 'I have to think calmly and sensibly how I can prevent this from happening to me.'

She felt as if she had been walking along a straight road and without any warning suddenly found a tremendous chasm in front of her.

'I will not panic,' she told herself, 'I will just find a way of escape.'

She knew, however, that it was a forlorn hope. How could she defy her mother's wishes, who would undoubtedly bring pressure to bear on the Duke to do what she planned because he needed the money?

Apart from that there was always the King as a last resort!

Susanna had heard in snatches of conversation how the King had assisted his special friends in marrying their daughters advantageously to the right sort of Noblemen.

"I said to the King," Susanna had heard her mother say once, "'you are so clever and so diplomatic, do help Vera marry that girl of hers to the Earl of Bexley. You know he will do anything you tell him. Just a word in his ear would make all the difference'."

"What did His Majesty reply?" Lord Lavenham had asked.

"Of course he was delighted for me to ask for his help," Susanna's mother answered. "He rather fancies himself as Cupid. And you must admit in a great many instances he has been extremely successful."

"Few people are brave enough to refuse the King anything he desires," Lord Lavenham commented somewhat cynically.

Susanna knew that her mother would not hesitate to ask the King's assistance if her plans for her to marry the Duke did not move towards a quick conclusion.

"I shall be married by the end of the Season!"

Susanna whispered the words and gave a little cry.

'I will go away,' she told herself. 'I will hide somewhere.'

It was lucky, if she really had to run away, that she had plenty of money.

There was never any difficulty in getting her mother's secretary to provide her with cash for the books she wanted to buy from shops where she did not have an account.

She had also found since she came to London that she liked to have money in her purse to give to the numerous beggars who held out skeleton-like hands as she crossed the pavement from the expensive dressmaker's shop into her father's luxurious carriage.

'They have so little and I have so much,' she would say to herself.

Surreptitiously, behind her mother's back, she would press a sovereign into some dirty hand and know by the expression of incredulous delight in a woman's dull eyes that she had given a fleeting happiness, if only for a moment, to someone very much worse off than herself.

'But if I do run away, I cannot sit back doing nothing,' she thought now, 'that would be impossible.'

Vaguely she thought that she might take a room somewhere and sit reading all day. Then she knew that was not really the solution to her problems, although she did not know what was.

On the fire stool beside her chair there were a number of newspapers.

Her father took both *The Times* and *The Morning Post* and usually read them at breakfast. The servants took them later to his study where he read them in the evening if he had time before dinner.

Susanna knew that it would raise a whole lot of questions if she took the newspapers away before he had finished with them. She therefore told the footman to bring them upstairs to the schoolroom the following morning.

They were a day old, but that did not really matter, since no one discussed the news with her or expected her to be interested in anything that did not concern clothes or people.

Now she picked up yesterday's *Times* and wondered if she could find employment of some sort, not because she needed money, but simply because it would fill the hours.

'Perhaps I could work in a library,' she mused.

Then she remembered that she might be seen by the very people she would wish to avoid.

'What I really would like,' she told herself, 'would be employment in one of the Art Galleries, although she had the uncomfortable feeling that in all the Galleries she had visited at one time or another the attendants had always been men.

'What can I do?' she asked and felt that she was really playing with the problem.

"I will not marry the Duke!" she cried aloud.

But she then thought that the solution did not lie in running away, but in facing her father and mother and telling them that she had no intention of marrying anyone she did not love.

Yet even as the idea came to her mind, she knew, looking as she did, that no one would love her and in her mother's Society love was an amusement that happened after marriage not before.

'What can I do? Oh! God, what can I do?' Susanna asked herself again and again.

She put *The Times* down on her knee. What was the point of searching for a job that did not exist except in her imagination.

Then, as she stared almost blindly at the paper wondering what else could help her, she saw a notice at the top of the Personal Column.

She read it almost without being consciously aware of what it said because her mind was elsewhere,

*"Wanted for someone temporarily blind, a reader prepared to travel abroad, who is proficient both in French and Italian. Apply between ten o'clock and noon, 96 Curzon Street."*

Susanna read the notice almost before it finally percolated into her mind. It struck her that this was something that she could do.

She certainly could read proficiently in French and Italian and then another sentence seemed to jump to her mind –

*"Prepared to travel abroad."*

If she was abroad, her mother would be unable to find her. She would not meet the Duke and so she would not be forced to marry him.

She read the advertisement again. It was crazy, she told herself, of course she could not do such a thing!

Then Miss Harding's words came back to her,

*"Help will come when you need it."*

This was the help she wanted! And if so, could she be so stupid as to refuse it when it was there waiting for her, even inviting her?

She felt that her heart was beating rather quickly and rose from the chair to walk to the window.

It was raining and the roofs of the houses stretching away interminably into the distance looked grey and depressing.

'That is the future for me,' Susanna told herself, 'unless somehow I can avoid it.'

Suddenly she made up her mind.

'I will go to 96 Curzon Street,' she told herself. 'If they accept me, then it will be meant, the helping hand I am waiting for. If I am refused, then I shall just have to think of something else.'

# CHAPTER TWO

Susanna climbed the steps of 96 Curzon Street and saw that it was a tall and imposing building.

The footman who had accompanied her from Lavenham House rang the bell and then stood back.

"Wait outside for me, James," Susanna told him. "I may be only a minute or I may be longer, I am not sure."

"Very good, miss," James replied.

He was a quiet lad from the country and Susanna had been glad that he was on duty when she came downstairs having made her plan of escape from the house.

Her mother never rose early and her father, having had his breakfast, would have already gone. The only danger therefore consisted of Mrs. Dawes, the housekeeper, who would think it extraordinary if she left the house alone and would undoubtedly tell her mother at once.

So Susanna decided that the only way she could answer the advertisement was to be accompanied by one of the footmen.

She had indeed hoped that James would be on duty and, when she reached the hall, she had said to him,

"I have to take a note to Curzon Street and, as it is such a nice morning, I should like to walk. Will you come with me?"

"Of course, miss. I'll just tell George to listen for the bell."

He hurried towards the pantry and came back with his high hat that he wore with his livery in his hand.

The Lavenham colours of dark blue and yellow were on his striped waistcoat and the Lavenham crest on the large buttons of his cut-away tail coat.

He looked very smart, Susanna thought, walking behind her and she knew that none of her mother's friends would think it in the least strange that she should be accompanied by a footman rather than an elderly maid.

What would have been scandalous was if she had walked even the short distance to Curzon Street alone and she thought, as she had often done before, how much she preferred living in the country where she could go anywhere she wished without a chaperone.

It was a day of clear sky with a blustery wind that made Susanna hold her fur-trimmed coat with one hand and her hat with the other.

It seemed to have a touch of adventure in it that made her feel that she was not doing anything outrageous but setting out on a voyage of discovery.

Then she told herself sensibly that there was every possibility that the job was already filled.

After all *The Times* she had read yesterday was a day old and already hundreds of suitable people might have rushed to answer such a tempting advertisement and one of them could have been accepted.

'Who would not want to travel abroad?' Susanna asked herself.

She had once been to Rome with her father and mother when they had been invited to stay by the Prince and Princess Borghese, who had children of the same age.

It had been a thrilling experience for Susanna and the Borghese children had shown their English visitors the sights of Rome with a somewhat condescending pride, insinuating that it was better than anything they could produce in England.

May had disliked their attitude, but Susanna had not cared. She had not listened to what the Italians said, as they were escorted round the huge remains of the Coliseum. She had been imagining what it was like when it was built.

There Roman Emperors had sat in all their glory to watch the fights of the gladiators and she visualised them in their graceful robes crowned with ivy and guarded by soldiers wearing the magnificent uniform of the Roman Legionaries.

She had been deep in her daydreams all the time she was in Rome until she was scolded by her mother for being dull and a bore.

"You must learn to talk, Susanna," she harangued her sharply. "It does not matter what you say, but try to make some sort of conversation. Anyone would think you were half-witted, as I am inclined to think you are, the way you just sit staring around you and saying nothing."

It had been impossible to tell her mother that she was carried away into the past, but she had told Miss Harding how deeply Rome had affected her and she had understood.

The door in front of her was opened and Susanna gave a little start.

A servant stood waiting for her to speak and after a moment's pause she said in a low voice, hoping that James would not overhear,

"I-I have come in – answer to the – advertisement."

He looked somewhat surprised and she thought that the reason must be her sable-trimmed coat, which looked too luxurious for someone in need of employment.

But she had nothing else to wear, for her mother had already made her throw away all the clothes she had owned before she came to London.

"This way, ma'am."

Susanna followed him into a marble-floored hall and up a curving staircase, which led to the first floor.

The servant opened a door and she was shown into an attractive sitting room, which looked out onto a little courtyard at the back of the building that had been converted into a garden although it was too early for any flowers to be in bloom.

"Will you please take a seat, ma'am," the servant said and left her alone.

Susanna looked round the room. It was well furnished in a somewhat masculine manner with comfortable armchairs instead of the imitation eighteenth-century French style that was found in most London drawing rooms.

One or two pictures on the wall Susanna could see were early Italian.

She wanted to have a closer look at them, but was afraid if someone came in and found her walking about the room they would think that she was inquisitive or perhaps impertinent.

The door opened and an elderly man came in. His hair was streaked with grey and there was a tired expression about his eyes as if he had been working hard.

As he walked towards her, Susanna rose to her feet.

"How do you do?" he began. "I understand that you have come in answer to the advertisement in *The Times*."

"That is right," Susanna answered, "but perhaps you have already found someone for the position?"

"We have, in fact, interviewed quite a number of applicants, but they were not, as particularly requested, proficient in either French or Italian."

"I speak both languages."

"Before we waste any more time, perhaps it would be advisable for you to do a small test. Are you agreeable to that?"

"Yes, of course," Susanna nodded.

"Then if you will come with me I will ask you to read some extracts to someone who you will not see but who will listen to you."

Susanna did not reply and after a moment the man added,

"I am afraid that I am somewhat remiss in not introducing myself. My name is Chambers and I am private secretary to a gentleman who has been injured in a motor car accident."

There was something in the way he said the last words that made Susanna reply instinctively,

"I am – sorry."

"You will understand that it is very tragic for a young man to know that he may lose his eyesight completely."

"Your advertisement said – 'temporarily blind'," Susanna murmured.

"That is what we hope," Mr. Chambers replied, "but I can explain everything to you later. Will you please tell me your name?"

"Yes, of course," Susanna replied. "I am – "

It suddenly struck her before she actually gave her name that it would be unwise to say who she was. Mr. Chambers and his employer might easily have heard of her father and, as her family name was Laven, it would be easy to connect the two.

"My – name," she said, "is Susanna – Brown."

It was the first name that came into her mind and even as she said it, she wished that she had been a little more imaginative.

"Will you come with me, Miss Brown?"

Mr. Chambers opened the door and they proceeded a little way along the passage before they went into another room. It was small and had another door opening out of it, which Susanna immediately suspected was a larger bedroom.

The room they were in, with its walls decorated with an attractive wallpaper and with colourful chintz curtains had been, she was quite certain before the bed had been removed, a dressing room.

Now there were a table and two comfortable chairs, one of which was very close to the communicating door.

She was not surprised when Mr. Chambers indicated it with his hand and said,

"Will you sit here, Miss Brown, and wait a moment."

Susanna sat down and Mr. Chambers went through the communicating door. She heard his voice speaking quietly to someone in the other room, but she did not hear a reply.

He then came back and handed her a copy of *The Morning Post*.

"Will you please read the editorial," he said, "and there will be no need for you to raise your voice any louder than usual."

He then went back into the other room and Susanna, feeling a little nervous, opened the newspaper and found the editorial on the centre page.

She was not nervous of reading aloud, only of the circumstances that she found herself in.

Miss Harding had always said that to read them aloud was the best way to revise the essays she had written on a number of different subjects.

"One gets the rhythm of what one has written when one reads aloud," she had told Susanna.

They also often read Shakespeare's plays to each other, Miss Harding taking some parts and Susanna others.

They later progressed to Milton and to *Childe Harold*, which Susanna had loved because she found Byron's verse inspired pictures in her mind.

The editorial she was to read was a warning about the continual efforts of the Germans to out-build the British Navy and an attack on the lassitude of those in Parliament, who were procrastinating in ordering the modern Battleships that the Navy required.

Thanks to Miss Harding, Susanna pronounced her words perfectly and her voice, although she had never thought about it, was deeper than that of most women and had a musical quality.

As she finished the editorial, she folded the newspaper back into shape and as she did so, Mr. Chambers came back into the room.

He smiled at her as if reassuringly and handed her a book. She took it from him and saw it was Voltaire's *Candide*, which, as she had read it with Miss Harding, she felt was an old friend.

"Read any part you like," Mr. Chambers told her and again left her alone.

She opened the book and chose a passage that had always amused her and read it with an elegant Parisian accent that her mother considered was so essential.

She had only read half the page when Mr. Chambers reappeared.

Susanna looked up at him, wondering if he had already decided that she was no use and did not wish her to waste any more of his time.

Before she could say anything he handed her another book saying,

"Your French is exceptional. Miss Brown, as I expect you have been told before."

"I am so glad you should think so," Susanna smiled.

"And we would now like to hear your Italian."

Mr. Chambers gave her a book that she did not know, but found when she opened it that it was a criticism of the Italian Classic Operas, comparing them unfavourably with the German.

Susanna did not agree with anything that the author said and she could not help her voice becoming somewhat critical and questioning as she read out what was written.

Again Mr. Chambers stopped her before she had read to the bottom of the page.

"Thank you, Miss Brown, that was excellent. Now Mr. Dunblane would like to meet you."

Susanna rose to her feet and followed Mr. Chambers through the open door to the next room.

As she had expected, it was a large bedroom. Two windows were hung with claret velvet curtains and the bed was upholstered in the same colour.

In the bed, lying back against a pile of pillows, was a man who appeared to be completely covered in bandages. He was almost like some mummy in an Egyptian tomb, Susanna thought, except that the bandages were white and new.

They gave him a strange appearance of being unreal or a creature from another Planet in an H. G. Wells novel.

Mr. Chambers walked towards the bed and, as Susanna followed him, he said to the man lying on it.

"I have Miss Brown with me, to whom you have just listened."

"You read well, Miss Brown," Mr. Dunblane said in a hoarse voice.

"Thank you," Susanna replied.

"I need someone to read to me as I cannot read for myself, being unable to see a *damned* thing!"

Susanna was startled both by the swear word and the bitterness in the bandaged man's voice.

"I am – sorry."

"I don't want pity!" Mr. Dunblane retorted almost rudely. "All I want is to be kept informed of what is happening outside the darkness that I am incarcerated in."

"Miss Brown understands," Mr. Chambers interposed soothingly, "but naturally she would like to know whether you are prepared to employ her."

"Of course I am prepared to do so," Mr. Dunblane replied sharply. "I could hardly be expected to tolerate those other idiots who could only speak the French of the gutter and the Italian of some ice cream merchant!"

Although he was speaking so scathingly, Susanna could not help giving a little chuckle of laughter.

"I amuse you, do I?" Mr. Dunblane asked. "Then I am glad that someone is amused. If you want to know what hell is like, try these bandages and learn what it is to sit in utter darkness."

As Susanna had no idea how to reply, she looked appealingly at Mr. Chambers.

"I will take Miss Brown away now, Mr. Dunblane," he said, "and arrange for her to accompany us when we leave tomorrow."

Susanna drew in her breath.

"You had better warn her what sort of person I am and that she must learn to put up with me!" Mr. Dunblane pointed out.

"I will do so," Mr. Chambers answered and moved towards the door.

As Susanna started to follow him, the man in the bed said unexpectedly,

"Goodbye, Miss Brown. I like your voice, which I suspect is more than you could say of mine."

"Goodbye, Mr. Dunblane, and thank you for employing me. I will try not to sound like an ice cream merchant!"

It was impossible to know whether she amused him or not, but she felt when she joined Mr. Chambers in the next room, that he was pleased with her.

They walked back to the sitting room that Susanna had been shown into originally.

"Will you sit down, Miss Brown," Mr. Chambers asked. "I feel that I should ask you a few particulars about yourself, although it is quite obvious that you are eminently suitable for the position."

"Thank you," Susanna said. "Are you really intending to leave London – tomorrow?"

"1 would prefer to do so," Mr. Chambers said, "for the doctors have ordered Mr. Dunblane to a warmer climate."

He saw the question in Susanna's eyes and added,

"He has a Villa outside Florence. He will be quiet and comfortable there and we can only pray that the operation which took place a few days ago will prove successful."

"What happened?" Susanna asked.

"Mr. Dunblane was involved in a motor car accident in America."

"In America!"

"He is, in fact, American."

"I had no idea. He speaks like an Englishman."

"Shall I say that Mr. Dunblane has had a cosmopolitan education?" Mr. Chambers replied with a smile. "English people always expect Americans to talk through their nose with a nasal accent, but as it happens Mr. Dunblane was at Oxford University and since then has lived more in Europe than in his own country."

"It must have been a very bad accident."

"It was and, although his body was badly bruised, his ribs fractured and his arms burnt in several places, it was his eyes that were most affected."

"It sounds horrible!" Susanna exclaimed.

"We brought him to England so he could be operated on at Moorfields," Mr. Chambers explained, "but the surgeons have now insisted that he remains completely in the dark for at least a month, perhaps longer. After that we shall know the best or the worst."

"You mean he might go totally blind?"

"I think I am right in saying," Mr. Chambers replied, "it is a fifty-fifty chance."

"I do hope the operation is successful."

"He has been operated on by those whom we believe to be the best surgeons in the world," Mr. Chambers informed her. "But you can understand, Miss Brown, that because of what he suffers and because of what he fears, Mr. Dunblane is not an easy man to live with."

"I can understand exactly what he is feeling. I think we would all feel terrified and desperate if we thought that we might never see the light again."

"Then I know you will make every allowance for him when he is depressed and disagreeable and sometimes, I am sorry to say, rude."

"I shall – understand."

"Now we must get down to more practical details," Mr. Chambers said briskly, drawing a small pad from his pocket. "I want to get Mr. Dunblane on the boat train from Victoria at ten o'clock tomorrow morning. He will find the journey to Florence very tiring, but I have arranged for private coaches to be attached to the ordinary trains and he will, of course, have his own servants with him."

"And a nurse I suppose?"

"Mr Dunblane insists on being nursed by his valet, who has had some training. He categorically refuses to have a woman fussing over him and I will be frank and tell you, Miss Brown, that if we could have found a man with the same qualifications as yourself, Mr. Dunblane would have preferred it."

"I must try not to be obtrusively feminine."

It was the sort of remark that Susanna would have made to Miss Harding. She thought that Mr. Chambers looked slightly surprised, but he made no comment and merely asked with his pencil poised,

"Have you a passport?"

"N-no, I am afraid not."

"Then I must procure one for you immediately. I am sure that there will be no difficulty. Perhaps you will give me your full name and address."

Susanna began to think quickly.

"My name," she said, "is Susanna Brown."

"Your parents?"

"They are both dead."

"I must have their names."

"Walter and Elizabeth Brown," she invented.

"And your address when your parents were alive?"

Again it was difficult, but finally she said because she knew it well,

"The Old Rectory, Lavenham Village, Hampshire."

"And your present address?" Mr Chambers enquired.

"I came to London last night after I had seen your advertisement," Susanna said. "I am staying with friends in Kensington."

"Previous to that?"

"I have been staying with – friends since my parents' death."

Mr. Chambers looked down at what he had written.

"I am afraid that I must have your date of birth," he said, "and I ought really to produce your birth certificate, but I am sure I can get round that difficulty."

He spoke in a manner that told Susanna he obviously had influence in official quarters.

She felt that it would be a great mistake to say how young she was, since if she was under twenty-one he would obviously expect her to have Guardians and be under their jurisdiction.

Quickly she made herself four years older than she was.

"I was born on July 2$^{nd}$ – 1885."

"Thank you, Miss Brown. Now would you like me to send a carriage for you in the morning or would you prefer to meet us at the Railway Station?"

"I think it would be easier for me to meet you at the Station," Susanna replied.

"Very well," Mr. Chambers said. "A servant will be looking out for you at the entrance at Victoria. If by any chance you miss him, ask for the private coaches of Mr. Fyfe Dunblane, which are attached to the boat train. I feel sure that any porter will know exactly where to take you."

"Thank – you," Susanna said faintly.

She had the feeling she was being swept off her feet and her future decided for her in a manner that, now it was actually happening, took her breath away.

Could she really do this? Could she really leave her mother and her father and start a new life on her own?

"Now you have forgotten something very important," Mr. Chambers broke into her thoughts.

"What is that?" Susanna asked apprehensively.

"You have not asked me what salary you will receive!"

"No, I am afraid I forgot."

"It's not very businesslike of you," he smiled, "for after all I am sure you will agree that 'the labourer is worthy of his hire.'"

"Yes – of course."

"I have advised Mr. Dunblane that the pay for anyone suitable is at the rate of twenty pounds per month, with, of course, everything provided."

"It seems very – generous," Susanna said.

She knew that was nearly twice as much as Miss Harding had received from her mother and she was surprised that she could earn so much.

"Well, now everything is settled and I can only hope that you will enjoy being in Florence."

"It is a place I have always wanted to visit," Susanna responded in all sincerity.

"I can promise you one thing, you will not be disappointed in Florence," Mr. Chambers replied.

He escorted her downstairs, shook her by the hand and a servant showed her out into the street where James was waiting.

"I am sorry to keep you so long, James," Susanna said as they walked away.

"That's all right, miss, it's nice to get a bit of fresh air."

As they crossed the road, she turned back a little to say to James who was a step behind her,

"I would be very grateful, James, if you will not mention where we have been to anyone. There was a friend I wanted to visit, but I don't think that her Ladyship would have approved."

She was well aware that it was wrong to intrigue with a servant against her mother, but she had to ensure that there were no questions asked about what she had been doing. If her mother's lady's maid learnt where she had been, it would instantly be reported.

As she walked on down the street, Susanna told herself that she was living in a dream and what had just happened was only a part of it and nothing true or substantial.

How could she really accept a position as a reader to a strange man?

How could she leave her home and go abroad to Florence, or anywhere else, without telling her father and mother and inevitably bringing a storm of protest and anger down on her head ?

But what was the alternative?

To stay and marry the Duke of Southampton?

She knew that her mother had not spoken idly when she said that she had chosen the Duke as a future son-in-law and whatever obstacles might arise she would get her own way.

'Mama always does,' Susanna told herself with a sigh, 'and, if she has the slightest suspicion that I am doing anything like this, she will prevent it even if it means that she has to lock me in my bedroom until the moment I walk up the aisle.'

"There is no use fighting Mama," Henry had said once when he had been forbidden to do something he longed to do. "She always wins. She is like a juggernaut that runs one over!"

It was a good description, Susanna thought, and she knew that she had been juggernauted by her mother all her life and it would be quite impossible for her to stand up against her now.

'All the same how can I go off on my own? It's a crazy idea!' Susanna thought.

But the alternative was to become like May, crushed, miserable and the property of a man who at least found her attractive, while the Duke –

Susanna had no need to speculate any further. She was well aware what the Duke would feel about her, fat plain and the last person who ought to be a Duchess.

She knew that apart from the Duke, people they would entertain on her money would snigger about her behind her back, even if they made a pretence of fawning to her face.

There was no loyalty amongst her mother's friends except on the principle of keeping up appearances.

In that they excelled in supporting each other and uniting in a common front against any criticism from the world outside their own particular circle.

'How can I do such a thing?'

'How can I?'

Susanna's footsteps seemed to echo the question over and over again.

But by the time she reached the front door of Lavenham House their refrain had changed,

'*I will do it! I will do it! I will do it!*'

*

Susanna reached Victoria Station soon after nine o'clock. She knew that she was early and, as she expected, there was no servant yet waiting outside the Station for her. However a porter escorted her to the private coaches attached to the boat train.

There were two of them and the Stewards seemed rather flustered that she should be here before anyone else. But when she apologised they found her a comfortable place to sit and brought her a cup of coffee and a plate of sweet biscuits.

She certainly needed something to still the agitation in her breast.

It seemed to her impossible that she had got away so easily and she knew that she would not feel really safe until the train had actually left the Station.

When she had gone back to the house yesterday morning with James, she had run upstairs to her bedroom and found, as she had hoped, the note she had put outside her door with *Do not Disturb* on it was still there.

This meant that she had not been called and no one except for James would realise that she had left the house.

She then undressed quickly, climbed into bed and rang the bell.

"I wondered what made you sleep so late, miss," the maid had said who came to draw the curtains.

"I awoke with a headache, Mary," Susanna replied, "and thought it best to sleep it off."

"Quite right, miss, and nobody's missed you, so to speak. Her Ladyship's not had her breakfast yet and I'll bring you yours."

"That would be very kind, Mary," Susanna had answered. "I am in no hurry to be up."

When she was dressed, it was to find that her mother intended to drive alone in Hyde Park and did not wish her to accompany her.

"I shall also be out for luncheon," Lady Lavenham said, "and if you have any fittings you had better take Mrs. Dawes with you. I am sick to death of your clothes and I cannot say that any of them do much for you!"

She looked disparagingly at her daughter as she spoke and Susanna said apologetically.

"I am afraid that is the truth, Mama, while the same gown on you would make you look as if you stepped straight down from Mount Olympus!"

Lady Lavenham was pleased at the compliment, but at the same time there was still a frown between her beautiful eyes as she looked at her daughter.

"I cannot think who you resemble," she reflected. "Your father's mother was a most distinguished-looking woman and mine, as you well know, was a beauty."

"Perhaps I am a changeling," Susanna murmured.

It was something she had often thought herself.

"It would not surprise me," Lady Lavenham snapped, "but the problem still remains as to what I can do to make you look more presentable."

"There is nothing, Mama, so I should forget about it."

"I wish I could," Lady Lavenham said. "Never mind, I have plans, so you can leave everything to me."

Susanna knew only too well what those plans were and the knowledge made her harden her heart when she later wrote a note to her mother.

It took her some time to decide what she should write before she began,

*"I have decided, Mama, that I am not suited for the Social world nor do I wish to marry anyone. I have therefore gone away to stay with friends and decide what my future will be.*

*I shall be quite safe and I do not wish you to worry about me and I promise you I can look after myself.*

*Please forgive me for any worry or anxiety I am causing you and do not try to find me, for I have no intention of returning home until the Season is over."*

Susanna thought that there were quite a number of other things she could say but, knowing her mother's dislike of reading long letters, she merely added,

*"With love both to you and Papa, I remain your affectionate daughter,*
*Susanna."*

She had thought of putting 'your affectionate and disobedient daughter', but decided that her mother would not find it amusing. Lady Lavenham had very little sense of humour.

Because her mother was out to luncheon and she was alone, it was easy for Susanna to carry out the next step, which might have been much more difficult.

She knew that as soon as she had finished in the dining room the servants would assemble in the basement for their own meal and this was her opportunity to carry her trunk down from the attic where it had been taken by the footmen after their arrival in London.

It was impossible for her to carry one of the larger leather-topped trunks, which weighed quite a considerable amount, but she could manage two smaller ones by sliding them down the stairs.

She took them into her bedroom and secreted them in the wardrobe, hoping that Mary would not see them if she laid out the afternoon dress that she should change into at teatime and then chose an evening gown to wear.

Once again luck was on her side because her father and mother were out for dinner and Susanna persuaded Mary to bring her up a tray with something light to eat at seven o'clock.

"I still have a bit of a headache, Mary," she said, "so don't disturb me. I will put the tray outside the door and then try to get some sleep."

"That's a good idea, miss, and I hopes you're not sickenin' for somethin'," Mary fussed over her. "It'd be terrible if you had measles or somethin' like that just when you're goin' to be presented to the King and Queen."

Susanna did not answer and Mary added,

"And her Ladyship'd be angry too if all those lovely gowns she's bought you are wasted!"

"I am sure I am not having measles," Susanna said, "just a tiresome headache. Perhaps it is something I have eaten."

"Too many chocolates, miss, gives one indigestion and makes you awful fat."

"I know, Mary, but I find I cannot resist them. Miss Harding used to scold me for being greedy."

"I expect you miss Miss Harding," Mary quizzed her.

"I do, I miss her terribly," Susanna agreed.

When she was alone, she wondered if she would not have been wiser to follow her first impulse and go to Miss Harding to tell her about her mother's plans for her to marry the Duke of Southampton.

But if she had done so, what could Miss Harding do about it? It was not really fair to burden her with her troubles when she had new pupils and a new place to cope with.

'She told me that I had to stand on my own two feet and look after myself and that is exactly what I am doing,' Susanna whispered to herself.

She locked the door and started to pack her trunks. She saw no reason why the clothes that had been paid for out of her own Trust should be left behind.

Besides, though she had a certain amount of ready money, she knew that it would be a mistake to be extravagant in case she intended to stay abroad after her employment with Mr. Dunblane came to an end.

She had gone to her mother's secretary as soon as Lady Lavenham had left the house and asked her for thirty pounds.

"Whatever do you want so much money for?" Miss McKay had asked.

"I have some books to buy," Susanna replied, "and a present I particularly want to give Mama and I want some gloves and a number of other things that are very expensive from a shop in Bond Street where we do not have an account."

"That's all right," Miss McKay said, "I did not mean to be inquisitive, but it just seemed a lot of money to carry about with you."

"I will not be carrying it for long," Susanna replied, "and then I shall be back again for more!"

"You're lucky there's more waiting for you," the secretary said. "The money that's spent in this house and at Lavenham Park at times makes my hair curl!"

"We are fortunate in that we can afford it," Susanna smiled.

"That's certainly the truth," the secretary replied.

Susanna had the idea that Miss McKay was rather envious and she thought that it must be a miserable life always handling other people's money when one had very little of one's own.

"I have a book in my bedroom. Miss McKay, that I think you might enjoy. I would like to give it to you," she then said.

"It is very kind of you, but I have no time for reading. When I get home at night, I have my old mother to look after. She is practically bedridden and I have to cook her a meal, clean the house and get everything ready to be back here first thing in the morning."

It was the first time that Miss McKay had spoken so frankly and Susanna felt guilty that she had always thought of her as a sort of automaton and not really a human being.

When she had gone upstairs to put the thirty pounds away in her purse, she had sat down at her desk and written a note to her father asking him to give Miss McKay twenty-five pounds of her own money.

*"She needs it, Papa, and I should be very grateful if you will carry out my wishes in this matter. Please forgive me for upsetting you and Mama, but I have to go away to think things over."*

She had a feeling that her father might understand better than her mother would, but she knew that, even if she had told him how much she hated the thought of having to marry the Duke, he would not support her.

He would merely have thought it extraordinary that as a woman she was not eager and willing to make a brilliant marriage.

Only when her trunks were packed and she had also filled a large hat box did Susanna climb slowly into bed.

She thought it unlikely that she would sleep because she knew that she had to rise very early to escape from the house when there was no one about.

In London her father usually breakfasted downstairs at nine o'clock when she would join him.

If she left the house at half past eight, she would have only the servants to contend with and if, as she anticipated, James and George were on duty in the hall, they would not query any orders she gave them.

It all worked out so perfectly that Susanna could hardly believe her good luck.

George was sent for a Hackney carriage, James carried her trunks downstairs and she had driven away before anyone could ask her a question or be astonished at what she was doing.

She was sensible enough to tell James that she wanted to go to Waterloo Station and only when they were well away from Lavenham House did she countermand the order and tell the cabman to drive to Victoria.

He accepted the change of direction without comment and Susanna over-tipped him in gratitude.

Now she was safely in the train and the only thing she could pray was that it would be on its way before anyone had any idea that she had actually left Lavenham House.

She had finished her coffee and all the biscuits when a Steward hurried past her saying to another,

"Here they come."

Susanna, feeling suddenly frightened and uncertain of herself, rose to her feet.

\*

Although Susanna had slept only a little the night before, she found it impossible to sleep as the train started on its journey across France.

The luxury they were travelling in seemed to her as unreal as everything else that she was doing.

There were Mr. Dunblane's own servants, four of them, besides his valet, Mr. Chambers and a rather superior man who seemed to combine the position of Courier and Major Domo.

It made Susanna feel as if she was a Royal personage travelling in a Royal train.

At Dover the Harbourmaster and a number of other Officials had supervised the carrying of Mr. Dunblane on a stretcher into a private cabin of the cross-channel Steamer.

There was also a single cabin for herself and doubtless another for Mr. Chambers and perhaps even the staff.

She was almost tired of being asked if there was anything she wanted and she wondered what Mr. Dunblane was feeling although she had not come into contact with him.

Susanna learnt that, although there would be a change of trains that drew their private carriages, they themselves would remain as they were until they reached Florence.

It was an excitement in itself to inspect the comfort of the drawing room she was to use and the bedroom that opened out of it. She knew that Mr. Dunblane was enjoying the same luxury.

There had been two carriages that they had travelled in to Dover, but three for the journey on to Florence, and there was no doubt that the Officials who saw them off were extremely impressed with the whole entourage.

'Mr. Dunblane must be very rich,' Susanna thought.

For she knew that apart from the King no one travelled in such luxury in Europe, whatever they might do in England.

She was aware that some of her mother's friends had private trains of their own in England, the Duke of Sutherland for instance, and other members of the aristocracy.

Her mother had often described to her the comfort of the Royal train that she and her father had often travelled on to Sandringham or to Warwick Castle, when with the King they enjoyed the hospitality of the beautiful Countess of Warwick.

But to cross Europe in such a manner was, Susanna thought, an experience that she must remember and she noted everything that happened, even standing at the window at small Stations to see the gaping expressions of those on the platforms.

It was a delight after she had dined alone with Mr. Chambers in her drawing room to undress in her bedroom, knowing that the large brass bedstead would undoubtedly be very uncomfortable.

She also found it easy to wash when the water came piping hot into the basin, which was covered when not in use by a red leather cover.

She climbed into bed and picked up one of her books she had brought with her. But she found it a little difficult to concentrate because there was so much to think about.

'I have run away! *I have really escaped*! And now it will take months for Mama and Papa to find me and by that time perhaps they will be reconciled to the fact that I will not marry anyone I don't wish to marry.'

She told herself that it doubtless meant that she would remain a spinster for the rest of her life.

Even if it was a depressing thought, she told herself that once she had established her independence she could perhaps do what she liked, travel or live on her own with no one to interfere with her.

She had the feeling that it was not going to be as easy as that, but she had at least taken a step in the right direction. And she had shown courage.

Miss Harding had said often enough that courage was the most important virtue anyone could have.

"Courage, not only to face life," she had said, "but also to know yourself. Most people are too frightened to look too deeply at themselves because they are apprehensive of what they will find. That is something you have to do, Susanna, and be brave about it."

'I have faced things frankly and honestly,' Susanna thought now. 'I know exactly what I am like – fat, ugly, unattractive, and it is unlikely that any man will be interested in me for myself. Therefore I have to make a life without men!'

She put down her book and threw herself back against her pillows.

'I am lucky, very lucky,' she reflected, 'I have money so I need not be afraid of poverty. By sheer chance I saw the advertisement in *The Times* and here I am setting out on a real adventure on my own and there is nobody, not even Mama, to stop me.'

# CHAPTER THREE

Susanna was deeply asleep when she became aware of a knocking on the door.

For a moment she could not think where she was and then the rumble of wheels beneath her told her that she was actually in the train travelling across France.

The knocking came again and she then sat up in bed, switched on the light and asked nervously,

"Who is – it?"

"It's Clint, miss, Mr. Dunblane's valet."

Susanna knew who he was without the explanation.

Mr. Chambers had already pointed out to her a small wiry-looking man who, he told her, was both valet and nurse to Mr. Dunblane.

"What is it?"

"Can I speak to you for a moment, miss?"

Susanna looked round her rather helplessly, wondering what she could do. Then, pulling the bedclothes a little higher so that they covered her, she called out,

"Perhaps you had – better open the – door."

The valet hardly waited for her to finish the sentence, but opened the door as she suggested. Standing in the aperture without making any effort to come into the compartment, he said,

"It's Mr. Dunblane, miss, he wants you."

Susanna looked at him wide-eyed.

"At this – time of the – night?"

"Night or day, it makes no difference to the Master, miss."

"No, of course — not."

"He wants you to read to him. In one of his moods, he is, and there's nothin' I can do for him."

"Of course I understand," Susanna agreed, "I will get dressed."

The valet hesitated a moment and then he said,

"I should not bother to do that, miss, as he wants you in a hurry. It's not as though he can see you."

"No, I see. Perhaps you will wait for me in the drawing room?"

"I will, miss, but I don't like to leave the Master alone for long when he's in the state he's in now."

"I will be very quick," Susanna promised.

As soon as the valet closed the door, she jumped out of bed and, picking up her dressing gown, which she had unpacked last night, slipped into it.

It was very pretty and warm, being made of rose-coloured velvet trimmed with bands of marabou. Her mother had almost bought it for herself and then when she had decided that she did not really want it, Susanna had been unable to resist anything quite so attractive.

She knew that it did not become her as it did her mother, nevertheless it was a reassurance now to know that it covered her discreetly.

When it was buttoned up to her throat and all down the front, she was as respectfully clothed as if she was wearing one of her day gowns.

Her hair was tied back in a bow at the nape of her neck and she made no effort to do anything with it, remembering that the valet had said in all truth that Mr. Dunblane would not see her.

Without really thinking she picked up the book she had been reading when she went to bed and carrying it in her hand hurried into the drawing room.

The valet was waiting for her, she thought impatiently, and he went ahead of her to open the door that led from her coach into the next.

As they stepped out onto the connecting passage, there was an increase in the noise of the wheels and in the cold air, which made Susanna glad to step safely into the next coach.

They passed through a drawing room exactly the same as the one in her coach and through another door into Mr. Dunblane's compartment.

Here was again a brass bedstead in the centre of it and the lights on either side of it revealed the mummy-like figure enveloped with bandages.

"Where the hell have you been?" Mr. Dunblane asked, as he must have heard the valet enter.

"I fetched Miss Brown as you told me to, sir. She's here and ready to read to you."

"Oh, she has come, has she?"

Although the tone of his voice was disagreeable, there was just an element of surprise in it.

"Yes, I am here," Susanna said quietly, "and, if I read to you, perhaps it will make you feel sleepy."

"Why should I want to sleep," was the reply, "I have done nothing but lie on my back all day and night! I have no idea whether I am in darkness or light, except I can hear Clint yawning his blasted head off!"

"I expect he is tired," Susanna said, "and I think it would be a good idea if he went to lie down while I read to you. I expect he has been on duty ever since we left Victoria Station."

Mr. Dunblane did not reply, but she had the idea that he had absorbed what she had said to him.

She looked round for a chair and, as Clint put one beside the bed, the occupant said,

"All right, Clint, get off with you. If I need you, I will ring the bell. You can hear it in your compartment I suppose?"

"It rings right beside my ear, sir," Clint answered, "and it would be ever so difficult not to hear it."

He spoke in a manner that Susanna knew her father would have thought over-familiar from his valet, but she had an idea that Clint, who had an American accent, was not the conventional valet, quiet and obsequious as was expected from every gentleman's gentleman!

She also thought that if he was responsible for the expertly tied bandages that covered his employer, he must be exceptional in other ways.

As Clint left, Susanna sat down on the chair and asked,

"What would you like me to read to you, sir?"

"Are there any books about the place?"

"I think I noticed quite a number in the drawing room," Susanna replied, "and I will fetch one unless you would like to listen to the one I have brought with me which I was reading before I went to sleep."

"Clint woke you up, did he?"

"Yes, but it does not matter. I am glad to do anything – you want me to do."

She had the feeling that he was going to retort, 'that is what you are here for,' and then prevented himself from saying it.

She opened her book, thinking as she did so that if Mr. Dunblane disliked what he was hearing he could always stop her. She thought however, that she had to explain,

"I was reading about Lorenzo the Magnificent." she began. "I felt it was appropriate I should know more about him before we reached Florence."

"Have you heard of him before?"

"Yes, of course."

"Why 'of course'? Most women, especially English ones, know little history and less about art."

"I hope I know quite a lot about both," Susanna replied, "and that is why it is more exciting than I can tell you, sir, to know that in Florence I shall be able to visit the Uffizi Gallery."

She thought as she spoke that she should add,

'If you will let me?'

There was silence for a moment and then Mr. Dunblane said disagreeably,

"I suppose like all women you are fancying that you look like Botticelli's Venus rising from the waves."

Susanna thought it was almost funny that he should think that.

If he could see her, he would know that she did not look in the least like Venus painted by Botticelli or anyone else. Even as she was about to tell him so, she changed her mind.

Why should she disparage herself to a man who could not see her? When the bandages were taken off, he would know all too soon what she really looked like.

It would perhaps be amusing when she knew him better to find out what sort of picture of herself she had created in his mind. And the same vice versa applied to her.

She could not see his features, he might be the ugliest man in the world or the most handsome. It was impossible to tell when he was swathed in bandages with only a hole that he could breathe through and another for speaking.

"I would certainly like to look like Venus," she said to him aloud. "But, as I have only seen a reproduction of Botticelli's famous picture, I shall be able to tell better if there is any resemblance once I have seen the original."

Then as she spoke a thought came to her that made her add,

"If I had the choice, I think I would prefer to look like Fra Filippo Lippi's *Madonna with the Laughing Angel*."

"Why?" Mr. Dunblane asked abruptly.

"I have seen a very fine reproduction of that picture," Susanna answered him.

She did not explain that it hung at Lavenham Park, and had been brought back from Italy by her grandfather.

"And the Madonna in that picture is your ideal of beauty?"

"It is not only because she is so beautiful," Susanna replied, "but because she looks so intelligent. You can see it in the height of her forehead and I think too in the expression in her eyes."

"So you want both beauty and brains," Mr. Dunblane remarked.

She thought as he spoke that he obviously did not believe that the two could go together.

"I think it must be very fortunate and very wonderful to be beautiful," Susanna said, "but to have brains is more satisfying and makes one appreciate life quite differently."

She had the idea that Mr. Dunblane was considering what she said and, because she did not want to continue the conversation about her being beautiful, she opened the book and said,

"I read last night about Lorenzo's family and how long it was before he earned the title of *Magnificent*, how he became interested in politics and had also made himself famous as an athlete.

*"Two days after the death of my father,"* he wrote in later life, *"although I, Lorenzo, was very young, being only in my twenty-first year, the principal men of the City and the State came to our house to condole on our loss and encourage me to take on myself the care of the City and the State, as my father and grandfather had done. This proposal being contrary to the instincts of my youthful age and, considering that the burdens and dangers were great, I consented unwillingly. But I did so to protect our friends and our property, for it fares ill in Florence with anyone who possesses great wealth without any control in the Government."*

Susanna paused and added,

"I think Lorenzo felt lonely and isolated. After all he was very young."

As she spoke she had almost forgotten that she was not talking over what she had read with Miss Harding in the way that they had always exchanged views.

"He was fortunate," Mr. Dunblane declared, "for it was not only his brilliance that gave him his great position, but he had faithful friends who rallied to him loyally."

"But he must have made them his friends by his own special qualities," Susanna argued. "If he had not had that unusual capacity for creating friendship, he would have been on his own."

She thought as she spoke of how few friends she had.

The girls who came to visit them in the country had always found May easier to get on with and she had invariably found herself the odd one out.

'It's not their fault,' she had told herself often.

It was because she found girls of her own age immature and usually incredibly boring. They giggled and simpered and they would talk only of clothes and things that they would do when they grew up.

Susanna thought that perhaps it was because she was so unattractive that these things did not appeal to her.

"Do you think that a man should rely so much on his friends?" Mr. Dunblane asked.

Because she had almost forgotten that he was there, she started.

"Of course he would have to rely on them, especially in situations such as Lorenzo faced. To have faithful friends is a compliment to oneself and there must be a great deal of satisfaction in that."

"You talk as if you wanted friends and have not many to compliment you in that way."

It struck Susanna that it was dangerous to talk about herself.

"Shall I go on?" she asked. "Lorenzo may have had friends, but he also had critics. Guicciardini for one, who said he 'desired glory and excellence above all other men and can be criticised for having too much ambition even in minor things. He did not want to be equalled or imitated even in verses or games or exercises and turned angrily on anyone who did so'."

"And what do you think about that?" Mr. Dunblane asked mockingly. "Do you not believe that a man should wish to excel and be first in anything he undertakes?"

"Of course men want to win at games and at sports," Susanna replied. "There is no racehorse owner who does not wish to win the Derby or a game shot who does not wish to bring down more pheasants than anyone else."

She was thinking of her father as she spoke and the enormous bags of birds that were killed at every shoot, starting with Sandringham where the King's personal record two years ago had been seven thousand, two hundred and fifty-six birds in four days.

"So you allow that a man should win in sport," Mr. Dunblane said, almost as if he was provoking her into an argument, "and what about his other achievements in life, a desire for a title, which is very prevalent in England and the fanatical struggle for money, which I expect you know persists in America? Surely all ambition is admirable?"

"I think it depends," Susanna answered, after thinking for a moment, "exactly what one is ambitious for. Self-glory must always be questionable unless the power aimed at is for the purpose of helping others like Politicians who should use their fame to benefit the country. And where money is concerned, Francis Bacon wrote, *money is like muck, no good except it be spread*."

Mr. Dunblane gave a little sound that she realised was a laugh.

"I see you have an answer for everything. Miss Brown," he said, "and I imagine our readings are going to force me to polish up my brains if they have not all been smashed out of me!"

As Susanna did not reply, he went on,

"But you have an unfair advantage, you can look up what you want to say, I can see nothing but darkness."

Again there was a note of depression in his voice which told Susanna that he was sorry for himself and he might at any moment revert to the railing against Fate which she was sure had made him send for her in the first place.

Aloud she said,

"I think perhaps Lorenzo is too controversial a subject for this hour of night, sir. I want you to listen to something different that I know by heart. Perhaps it will help you to relax and go to sleep, which I think you – ought to do."

"Are you worried about me?"

"But, of course, like everyone else around you. We want to get you well and, although I am no doctor, I have always been convinced that to cure one part of the body every other part must co-operate in the healing process."

"What do you mean by that?"

"Our bodies are like a machine," Susanna replied, "if one piece of it goes wrong, then it is easy to bring the whole thing to standstill."

"I understand what you are saying. Go on with your recitation and I will try not to be intelligent about it."

Susanna had not thought until that moment exactly what she would recite, but she decided quickly that it should be Byron's *Stanzas written on the Road between Florence and Pisa*.

She began in her soft musical voice,

*"Oh, talk not to me of a name great in story,*
*The days of our youth are the days of our glory,*
*And the myrtle and ivy of sweet two-and-twenty*
*Are worth all your laurels, though ever so plenty."*

She said the lines quietly and thought as she did so that she had never dreamt when she had learnt them with Miss Harding that she would be on her way to Florence and that the City which she had longed to see would be waiting for her!

The words seemed very appropriate at this moment, but she wondered as she continued verse after verse what her mother would think if she knew where she was, reciting in a fast-moving train to a blind man swathed in bandages while she was sitting beside his bed wearing only her dressing-gown!

Only as she said the line, '*I knew it was love and I felt it was glory*', did she think that perhaps she should have chosen some other poem.

There was no doubt that it was extremely reprehensible to speak of love to a man she did not even know!

Then she realised that Mr. Dunblane was asleep.

She could hear his quiet even breathing and it was obvious too by the way that he was now relaxed with his head turned a little sideways on the pillow that her recitation had had the effect that she desired.

Very quietly she rose to her feet, moved out of the compartment and with a little difficulty managed to get back to her own drawing room and through that to her bed.

Only as she snuggled down again against the pillows and pulled the sheets over her shoulders, did she think that this was the most extraordinary thing that had ever happened to her.

Even May or Miss Harding would find it hard to believe it if ever she told them.

'I wonder what he looks like?' she questioned and had arrived at no answer before she fell asleep.

*

The next day was so exciting that the hours seemed to speed past as quickly as the train itself was moving.

Whenever she was not required to read to Mr. Dunblane, Susanna would sit in the drawing room looking out through the window anxious not to miss one glimpse of France as they thundered through it.

The huge cultivated fields without hedges or boundaries, so unlike England, were an enchantment in themselves.

The small villages each dominated by the spire of a Church were a joy and even the larger Stations with their platforms packed with people, who looked so different from those she had seen elsewhere, were an absorbing interest.

Because she thought it absurd to feel self-conscious about telling Mr. Dunblane what she could see, she talked about the countryside that they were passing through, looking out of the window of his compartment to describe the forests, the bullocks working in the fields and the peasants and their children.

When eventually they passed through the Alps, she found it impossible to repress her excitement at the sight of the snowy peaks and the deep shadowing valleys beneath them.

Mr. Dunblane did not tell her that he had no wish to hear what she could see although occasionally he spoke bitterly and in a manner that told her that he was suffering agonies of fear that he should be blind for ever.

She thought about him and finally he gave her the opportunity of saying what was in her mind.

It was on the evening of the second day and, as darkness fell, and it was impossible for Susanna to see anything more through the window, Clint came in to draw down the blinds.

"I presume it's dark," Mr. Dunblane said in a disagreeable tone as the valet left.

"Yes, it's dark," Susanna replied, "and so the Cook's tour, which I am giving you, of a journey to Florence, will have to wait until tomorrow."

He did not reply and after a moment she said,

"You must – tell me if you would – rather I did not talk about what I can see."

"As I may have to use your eyes or someone else's for the rest of my life, I might as well get used to it!" Mr. Dunblane answered her savagely.

He paused a moment before he continued,

"You are so busy being imaginative. Have you ever tried to imagine what it would be like if you were blind? If you sat in darkness and had to accept second hand descriptions of everything you longed to see for yourself! "

"If that happened to me," Susanna replied, "I hope I should have the sense and the courage – to develop my *Third Eye*."

"What the hell do you mean by that?"

The question was so rough as to be almost violent and Susanna felt herself tremble a moment before she went on bravely,

"Have you never heard of the *Third Eye*? The Egyptians knew all about it."

"Are you talking about the Cyclops, who I thought were monsters and if I remember correctly only had one eye in the middle of their foreheads?"

"No, I am not talking about them, but the Ancient Egyptians when they were at the height of their glory and their Priests understood mysteries that were kept for the initiated or the Pharaohs."

"I suppose you had better tell me about them," Mr. Dunblane muttered surlily.

"They indicated the *Third Eye* on the statues of their Gods by a knob on the forehead," Susanna began. "They trained people in the use of this psychic centre in the ancient temple of Ma-at."

She paused a moment to see if Mr. Dunblane would say anything and, when he did not, speak she went on,

"The God of Ma-at was vulture-headed because vultures have a sight so keen as to be almost clairvoyant. When people responded to the training of the Priests, they became seers or psychics."

"A lot of damned nonsense!" Mr. Dunblane murmured.

Susanna ignored his remark and went on,

"The seers could see with their trained *Third Eye* right through the body, as an X-ray does, and diagnose disease. All over the East I believe you can find statues with a knob on the forehead indicating the *Third Eye*."

Her voice had a lilt in it now as she went on,

"When I first read about it, I went with my Governess to the British Museum and we found several statues with a knob on their foreheads. It was very exciting!'

"You think that is what you would get if you developed your *Third Eye*?" Mr. Dunblane asked scornfully.

"No, but I think everybody has the capacity to use their own intuition but most people neglect it."

"In what way?"

"When you engage a servant, do you judge him on what you see or feel about him or do you rely entirely on his references?"

"I want references and they had better be good ones!"

"Then you have let your *Third Eye* grow lazy and inactive," Susanna said. "And surely you have met people whom you have liked instinctively and found them very congenial, almost as if they have meant something in your life before."

"I cannot think of anyone."

"Then perhaps you have hated someone for no good reason; disliked them as soon as they came into the room. There might have been nothing unusual about them on the surface and yet your instinct told you that they were untrustworthy and perhaps wicked."

"How are you suggesting that I should develop this rather doubtful quality?"

"I think this is a great opportunity," Susanna replied, "because at the moment you cannot judge by what you see and therefore what you feel is intensified. For instance what do your vibrations think of mine while we are talking to each other?"

She was not being personal but was merely developing her argument as she had done so often with Miss Harding.

"Tell me what you feel," her Governess had often said. "Not what your brain tells you you should think about it, but how your subconscious, if you like, reacts."

"If you want compliments," Mr. Dunblane said, "I am not going to give them to you!"

"Oh! I did not mean it like that," Susanna exclaimed almost in horror, "and you are accusing me of being feminine – which I am not!"

"Why not?"

"For a lot of reasons, but mostly because Mr. Chambers said that you did not really want a woman in this post. However, as there were no other applicants who had any qualifications, I promised him that I would not be aggressively feminine and it is something I have no intention of being anyway."

"But you are still a woman whether you like it or not!"

Now his voice was amused.

"Something that has never troubled me in the past and certainly does not concern me in the future."

"That is a ridiculous statement, but I presume by the way you speak, you have never been in love."

"No, of course not!"

"Why so vehement? It will happen one day and then you will marry and settle down and doubtless have a large family of tiresome children."

"I shall never marry!"

"Why ever not?"

"For reasons that are my – own."

Susanna closed her book with a little snap and added,

"I think it is time for me to get ready for dinner, I would not wish to keep Mr. Chambers waiting."

"Chambers can wait if I wish him to!"

Susanna had risen to her feet.

"That is a very selfish remark," she said, "and you are obviously not using your intuition about him. He is almost killing himself worrying about you and so I think you should be grateful."

Only as she went from the compartment before Mr. Dunblane could reply did she think that it was not at all the way that she should have spoken to her employer.

'Perhaps he will send me home immediately we arrive,' she thought apprehensively.

But she knew because she was using her intuition that the conversations when they seemed to duel with each other had, if nothing else, roused him from the dull despair that he was feeling when they had started out on the journey.

Now already he spoke more quietly and she could feel that he responded to her even when she made him angry.

'All the same, I must be careful,' she told herself. 'I could not bear to be sent back to England doubtless without a reference.'

As she went to bed that night, she found herself thinking over the conversations that she had had with Mr. Dunblane during the last two days and hoping that when they reached Florence there would not be dozens of other people to talk to him.

Then she remembered that Mr. Chambers had said that he was to be quiet and that was a consolation in itself.

'I must think up new ideas and I must stimulate his mind. I must somehow make him rise above his physical sufferings.'

She did not quite know how she could do so, but she felt that was what she should try to do.

'One thing,' she thought, 'there will be plenty to talk about in Florence.'

Then she felt her heart leap at the idea of viewing the pictures that she had always longed to see and naturally Florence itself, which her books had told her was one of the loveliest places in the whole world.

\*

Susanna awoke early because it was impossible to sleep knowing that they had arrived and the sun, which was creeping beneath the curtains in her bedroom, was shining over the City where four centuries ago Lorenzo the Magnificent had reigned supreme.

She had remembered reading in a book in the library at Lavenham Park that Florence was not only famous for

Palaces and Churches, which were so much part of its history.

*"Florence is the bells in the morning,"* she read, *"the moon coming up over the San Miniato, the narrow streets that are hardly more than slots, the over-hanging eaves of the Palaces and the clop-clop of the donkeys coming into the market in the early dawn."*

That was the Florence she wanted to see besides the Florence of the sculptures, the pictures and the buildings that she had seen rising above them as they drove through the streets after arriving late last night at the Railway Station.

She had thought then that the smell of Florence was different from what she had known anywhere else.

She thought that she could distinguish the fragrance of the mauve wisteria that hung over many of the walls, the aroma of roasting coffee and the damp wet smell that came from the River Arno as they drove beside it.

Mr. Chambers had already told her that Mr. Dunblane's Villa was not in the City but a little way outside on a hill.

There were hills all around Florence covered with cypress trees pointing like dark fingers up to the sky.

Susanna was speechless when they reached the Villa and she saw how beautiful it was.

Mr. Chambers told her that once it had been a Convent and Mr. Dunblane's father had changed it into a Villa where he had spent the remaining years of his life.

She was entranced by the long white building with its tiled roof that seemed to radiate holiness and also a mystery that was an intrinsic part of Florence.

"His father's collection of pictures and furniture has made the Villa one of the finest private homes to be found anywhere in Italy," Mr. Chambers had told her. "And the garden, which he devoted himself to until he died, is beautiful beyond description."

'I must see it,' Susanna told herself now and jumped out of bed to pull back the curtains to find her breath taken away by the stunning view that she could see from the window.

There rising above the houses was the huge dome of the Cathedral, which had been built by Brunelleschi in 1420 and, as she had read, *"it had to reach such a height and magnificence that one could not expect anything more noble* or *more beautiful from human handiwork."*

But that had been a long time ago and she had not expected to see it still dominating the whole of Florence and to feel, as had been intended all those years ago, to lift her heart into the sky.

Then she saw the garden. It was a blaze of colour and there were flowers that appeared to have come from Heaven itself, even though they had been planted by human hands.

"It is lovely! *It is so lovely*!" Susanna exclaimed.

Because she could not wait to see more she washed in cold water and started to dress herself.

She realised with delight that she could put away all the thick dresses she had worn in London and could wear one of the cool thin gowns that her mother had bought her in anticipation that the weather in June and July might be very hot.

She slipped out of the Villa, which seemed very quiet, although she was certain that the smiling Italian servants, who had greeted them when they arrived last night, were already busy in the kitchen.

Mr. Dunblane had been too tired to do anything but, Clint told her with satisfaction, fall asleep as soon as he was in bed.

She and Mr. Chambers had dined alone at an old refectory table in a room that once must have exuded the austerity of a Convent.

Now with the floor covered with magnificent rugs, the walls hung with tapestries and lit with huge candles in gold carved candlesticks that might once have stood in a Church, it had an opulent beauty.

Other rooms were even more breathtaking, Susanna had discovered, but she had been too tired to see many of them last night.

"Go to bed, Miss Brown," Mr. Chambers suggested. "You will have plenty of time to explore everything tomorrow. I know you must be tired."

"I am a little," Susanna admitted. "It must be the constant vibration of the train."

"I would like to thank you," Mr. Chambers said unexpectedly, "for the way that you have kept our patient interested during what has undoubtedly been a long and exhausting four days."

Susanna looked please and he continued,

"I am convinced that it is very bad for him to work himself up, as he did all the way across the Atlantic, into an angry despair, railing against Fate and refusing to be optimistic about the future."

"I have tried to help him."

"And you have done so. I can only think that we were very lucky after so many disappointments to find you."

He must have thought that Susanna looked surprised for he added,

"The advertisement had been in *The Times* for three days before you came to us."

He smiled as he went on,

"I was getting extremely tired of hearing applicants mispronounce the simplest French words and I know that Mr. Dunblane felt the same."

"I am sorry for him."

"If he regains his eyesight in the end," Mr. Chambers commented, "perhaps what has happened will do him good."

"Do him good?" Susanna queried.

"Everything in his life has gone right for him up to now. He had been a golden boy in more ways than one."

"Like Lorenzo the Magnificent," Susanna said without thinking.

Mr. Chambers laughed.

"I daresay you are right and you must look at the terracotta bust of Lorenzo by Verrocchio. It is one of my favourite works of art."

"I would love to see it."

"Then I promise you that I will make arrangements as soon as we are settled in to take you into the City and I know without asking that you want to visit the Uffizi Gallery."

"Of course!"

She had gone to bed feeling excited. There was so much for her to see and now, as she stood in the sunshine in the garden gazing at the view, she realised that her imagination had failed to envisage even a tenth of the wonder of it.

She walked further into the garden looking at the flowers with delight until she remembered almost guiltily that her employer would not be able to see them.

She bent down to pick a few sweet-scented lilies which were so delicate and exquisite it seemed strange that they should be related to the huge arum lilies that one always associated with the decoration of Churches or even the more graceful bell-shaped Madonna lilies.

Those she had picked, Susanna thought, were like tiny angel voices that could hardly make themselves heard in a Church choir.

Then she felt shy because she had been whimsical.

'Everything is so beautiful,' she told herself, 'that I must remember that I am the only ugly feature in a picture of translucent loveliness that could only be captured by a Master.'

She was not complaining, she thought, about her own appearance, she was only using her common sense to prevent herself from being carried away into an ecstasy that she was not really entitled to.

She walked round a clump of shrubs covered in blossom and saw to her surprise a large swimming pool. At least that was what she supposed it was, for she had never seen one before.

She would have thought that it was merely an artificial pond if it had not been lined with blue tiles and surrounded by flagstones. Also the water was moving constantly and it was so clear that she could see the bottom.

"Are you intending to have a swim, Miss Brown?" a voice asked her and Mr. Chambers joined her.

"I thought it must be a swimming pool." Susanna said. "I have heard that Americans have them in their gardens in America, but I have never actually seen one before."

"Mr. Dunblane's father put one in when he converted the Villa," Mr. Chambers explained.

"Do you swim?"

"I used to when I first came here," he replied, "but now I find it rather tiring so I leave such strenuous exercise to young people like yourself. You will find the water warm even at this hour of the morning."

"Oh! I could not swim here," Susanna said quickly, "though I did learn to swim when I was a child in the lake at my home."

"No one will see you," Mr. Chambers answered, "and, as we try to provide our guests with everything they require, you will find a number of bathing dresses in the pavilion on the other side of the pool. Don't be shy. Have a dip whenever you feel like it."

"Thank you, I will think about it."

She knew as she spoke that she would be far too shy to go into the pool being well aware how fat and ungainly she would look in a bathing dress.

She had seen fat old women bathing at Brighton when she and May have gone there once to convalesce after having whooping cough.

They had laughed at the spectacle people made of themselves bobbing up and down in the waves and

Susanna knew that she would hate to be laughed at in the same manner.

'At the same time,' she thought a little wistfully, 'I would love to swim in that beautiful pool.'

Although Mr. Dunblane would not see her, Mr. Chambers might do so, besides Clint and all the servants.

'No! It is something I will never do,' she told herself resolutely.

Carrying her lilies she walked back with Mr. Chambers to the Villa and found that breakfast was waiting for them on a sheltered verandah with a different view of Florence.

Now there was the Arno glittering in the sunshine, spanned by many bridges and she could see clearly the oldest and most famous of them, the Ponte Vecchio.

'How can I ever be grateful enough for being here?' she asked with a little throb in her voice.

Almost as if it was in answer to her question, Clint came into the room.

"The Master wants you at once, Miss Brown," he said. "He feels he's bein' neglected."

"Oh! dear!" Mr. Chambers exclaimed, "I should have gone to see him before I had my breakfast."

"There is no hurry for you, sir," Clint said. "It's the young lady he's askin' for and it's best not to keep him waitin'."

"No – of course not," Susanna said.

She had not finished her breakfast, but she jumped up from the table and, picking up the little bunch of lilies, followed Clint along the cool passages and through a lovely courtyard surrounded with cloisters into an enormous bedroom.

On a dais there was a bed, draped with curtains which fell from a high carved corona of flying angels and beneath them on the bedhead was an enormous Coat of Arms emblazoned with colour.

Below it Mr. Dunblane looked very strange and unreal enveloped in his bandages

"Where have you been?" he asked sharply. "No one has come to see me, although I suppose that you and Chambers were enjoying yourselves in the sunshine."

"I have been looking at the view and exploring the garden and found your swimming pool," Susanna said. "It is all like a Fairy story."

"If you are envisaging yourself as the Princess in it, I must point out," Mr. Dunblane said, "that the Prince is being somewhat neglected."

"I am sorry," Susanna said, "but as it is still very early, I thought that you would be asleep."

"Sleep! Sleep! That is all anyone wants me to do. Nobody cares if I lie rotting in my bed as long as they can enjoy themselves."

"That is not true and you know it," Susanna pointed out in her soft voice. "However grumble away if you want to, I am here to listen to you."

"I suppose you were going to say that you are paid to do so, you are – "

"I was not going to say that, but now you mention it, the answer is yes!"

Mr. Dunblane gave a little laugh

"Damn you. You never allow me to be really sorry for myself."

"Why should I when you have so much to be grateful for."

"What?"

"I am not going to reply to that question," Susanna answered. "You can count your mercies as well as anyone else and what has happened to your *Third Eye* this morning?"

"It's not there!"

"That I do *not* believe. So we will try and see if it works. Tell me what these are."

She bent forward as she spoke and held the lilies a little way from the hole in the bandages that he breathed through.

"Did you pick them in the garden?" he asked.

"Yes, of course," Susanna answered, "and, as they are small and insignificant, I thought that they would be gratified to be allowed to come and see you while their more flamboyant friends were left outside!"

Mr. Dunblane laughed again.

"You are an amazing woman! Well, you can earn your keep by reading me the newspapers if they have arrived, before I tell you when you can go and look at your own face in the Uffizi Gallery."

Susanna drew in her breath.

If he only knew what she really looked like, she thought. Then she told herself that she would not spoil her own happiness and her own delight in being in Florence by telling him the truth.

How amid such loveliness could she bear to say?

'I am plain, ugly and fat!'

"When you do allow me to visit the Uffizi," she said aloud, "I will tell you whom I most resemble, Simonetta Vespucci, the model for Botticelli's Venus, or the intelligent young lady who sat for Fra Filippo Lippi."

She paused before she added,

"I have read that she may have been Lucrezia Buti, who ran away from a Convent to be with the artist."

"Of course you must not forget to recognise me in Lorenzo the Magnificent," Mr. Dunblane said.

"Naturally," Susanna agreed. "The things Mr. Chambers has told me about you makes me quite certain that you were Lorenzo in a previous incarnation."

She spoke mockingly and Mr. Dunblane said suspiciously,

"I suppose that far from flattering me you are predicting that eventually I shall fall from grace and, apart from financial difficulties, succumb to gout."

"That is a long way ahead."

"In the meantime my sins have caught up with me in another form of punishment."

"Now you are being morbid, sir," Susanna retorted. "How can your accident have anything to do with your sins?"

"Perhaps like Lorenzo, I was puffed up with pride and determined to be first in everything I undertook. Surely you would say that the punishment fitted the crime?"

"I should say nothing of the sort," Susanna answered almost crossly. "I think this sort of introspection is very bad for you, so I will read you the news."

She saw that beside the bed there was an Italian newspaper and an American one. The Italian was a week old and she thought that it must have travelled with them from England.

"There are two newspapers here," she said. "Which would you prefer first, the Italian or the *New York Times*?"

"You have the *New York Times*," Mr. Dunblane exclaimed. "Why have you not read it to me before?"

"For the very good reason that it was not given to me," Susanna replied.

"Well, read it now! Turn to the sporting pages and see if there is anything about the motor car trials."

Susanna looked at him in surprise. For the first time she thought that perhaps his accident had something to do with motor racing.

Mr. Chambers had not mentioned it and she had thought in her mind that he had been involved in an ordinary road accident such as took place quite frequently since motor cars had appeared on the roads.

Despite the fact that motor cars were restricted to travelling at sensible speeds they frightened the horses who often plunged about in their terror, upsetting the carriage that they were attached to and occasionally with disastrous consequences.

Quite a number of her mother's friends travelled about London in an electric Brougham and her father had talked of buying a motor car in which they could reach the country more quickly than they did behind his thoroughbred horses. This was very different, Susanna knew, from the motor car races that she believed, although she was vague about them, had been part of the American development of the vehicle.

Henry was the one person in their family who was really thrilled by motor cars. In fact when he was home from Eton he talked about little else.

Now, thinking back, Susanna had always been a good listener to her young brother's enthusiasms and now she recalled his telling her that the previous year a Stanley Steam Car had reached an incredibly high speed on Daytona Beach.

As she tried to find the sports page of the *New York Times*, not being familiar with that newspaper, she wondered, as Mr. Dunblane had, why it had not been given to her before.

It was difficult as she glanced down the page to find anything about motor cars and then at last, she discovered it.

"Oh! here it is," she exclaimed at length.

"What does it say?" Mr. Dunblane asked and Susanna read aloud,

> *"There is no doubt that Felice Nazzaro's Fiats, which dominated the major races this year, are expected to win the Targa Florios. Although Louis Coatalen, an expatriate Frenchman, has designed a 25 HP Hillman for the 190 TT."*

"Is there nothing about American motor cars?" Mr. Dunblane asked sharply.

Susanna looked quickly down the next few paragraphs and then read out,

> *"It is anticipated that the world's first supercharged car, a six cylinder Chadwick, will be seen in the new American Grand Prix race in Savannah and*

*Robertson's Locomobile is tipped to win the Vanderbilt Cup."*

"What else?" Mr. Dunblane asked in a voice that was surprisingly urgent.

"*America is now very prominent in the motor world, her car production having exceeded that of France in 1906. Falcons have swept the market so far, but it is whispered that Henry Ford has put into production an amazing Model T, an ultra-simple, almost totally indestructible vehicle, which will bring reliable motoring within nearly everyone's reach.*"

Before Susanna finished speaking, Mr. Dunblane gave a cry that was almost a scream.

"Why was I not told this? Why the devil has it been kept from me?" he asked furiously. "Get Chambers, tell him to come here immediately!"

He spoke so loudly and so fiercely that Susanna instinctively rose to her feet.

"Go on, fetch him! What the hell are you waiting for!" Mr. Dunblane now bellowed.

Frightened at his violence Susanna ran from the bedroom to find Mr. Chambers.

# CHAPTER FOUR

Susanna was on the terrace staring at the view when an hour or so later Mr. Chambers came and joined her.

He was carrying a large pile of papers in his hand and she turned to say,

"I am sorry – very sorry if I – upset him."

"It was my fault," Mr. Chambers replied. "I brought the *New York Times* from London and very stupidly left it in the sitting room. Clint picked it up and thought that I intended for Mr. Dunblane to have it."

"He seemed to be upset because Mr. Henry Ford is bringing out a new car," Susanna said, "and I thought perhaps he had investments in other makes."

She had been thinking as she was waiting that American fortunes that were made so quickly could doubtless disappear at the same speed.

Her father had spoken of disastrous financial crashes on Wall Street and she remembered once a terrible commotion because some of his friends had invested in a gold mine in which the seam ran out.

"It is something like that," Mr. Chambers replied and Susanna felt that he did not wish her to ask any more questions.

'It is no concern of mine,' she told herself. 'At the same time, if Mr. Dunblane loses a great deal of money he might have to sell this wonderful Villa and would certainly not be able to live in the comfort he enjoys now.'

"I think Mr. Dunblane would like you to go back to him," Mr. Chambers said, "and I suggest that after luncheon, while he rests, we go into Florence and you can have a quick look at some of the pictures that you are longing to see."

"Can we really do that?" Susanna asked excitedly.

"We will try," Mr. Chambers promised, "although if Mr. Dunblane wants you I am afraid that we shall have to wait until another day."

Susanna hurried back to Mr. Dunblane's bedroom and, when she knocked on the door and he called out 'come in', she found to her surprise that he was not in the huge curtained bed, but sitting in an armchair by the window, which was wide open.

"Oh, you are up," she exclaimed, "I am so glad. I am sure it is important for you to breathe this lovely warm air."

"Stop fussing about me," Mr. Dunblane replied, "and if you have something positive to 'soothe my fevered brow', I should like to hear it."

Susanna looked at him a little nervously, feeling that he was still upset.

She had automatically picked up several books on her way to his bedroom and, because she was so excited with the idea of visiting Florence, she had not looked at them very carefully.

Now she saw that one was the book that she had read to him before about Lorenzo the Magnificent and she felt that perhaps they had exhausted their conversation on that subject. Instead she looked quickly at the others to find something different that would interest him.

Then surprisingly he said,

"I have changed my mind. Talk to me, tell me about your life and why you have to earn your living."

It was fortunate that he could not see the startled expression in her eyes.

"You will find that a very boring subject," she replied evasively. "I would much rather talk about you or this wonderful Villa that your father has made so perfect."

There was no response to this and after a moment she said,

"I would also like you to tell me about Florence. When people speak of a place they know, it is always so much more interesting than a guide book."

"I have a feeling," Mr. Dunblane said, "and now I am using my *Third Eye*, that you are deliberately luring me away from what I want to know about you. Why should you be mysterious unless you are hiding something?"

Susanna thought that he was actually becoming far too perceptive.

"I cannot – imagine why you should – think that."

"Your voice is very revealing, Miss Brown. When you are nervous, as you are now, because you think that I am delving too deeply into something you don't wish me to know, the whole tone changes. I suppose hundreds of people have told you that you speak like music."

"No one has – told me – that," Susanna murmured.

"Then they must have been deaf," Mr. Dunblane said, "or because I am blind, I am for the first time in my life, using my ears as they should be used."

"Or, as you said yourself, it might be your *Third Eye*."

"I have been thinking about that. It seems extraordinary that no one has ever spoken to me about it before, although I suppose that there must be quite a number of people, even in this enlightened age, who know about it."

Susanna smiled as she responded,

"I have read that there are esoteric schools, or there were, in different parts of the world which were attended by all the great leaders of creative thought."

"That is as far-fetched as the claim of Madame Blavatsky that there are Masters hidden in the Himalayas who are there to teach and guide the people who believe in them."

The scathing way he spoke made Susanna say,

"You are quite obviously one of the unbelievers."

"Of course," he replied. "I think it is a great deal of nonsense thought up by frustrated women who have nothing better to do."

"And yet we know that all the great innovators like Buddha, Plato and Christ," Susanna said, "spoke to their disciples in a way their ordinary followers would not have understood."

"How do you know that?"

"I can quote you a number of instances in the Bible if you wish me to do so."

"I think you have been deceived and deluded by a lot of rubbish that has no reality in fact and would be laughed at by any person with any intelligence."

Susanna thought for a moment and then she said,

"Then you don't believe in miracles?"

"I have never seen one myself."

She hesitated before she went on,

"You have just been in a very bad motor car accident. You don't think it a miracle that you were not killed? Why did you survive what might have been fatal for a less fortunate man?"

Even as she spoke she was almost astonished at herself for saying anything so personal and yet the words seemed to come to her lips almost without her conscious volition.

There was a long silence before Susanna said in a nervous little voice,

"Forgive me – I should not have – said that. I have no wish to – upset you again."

"You don't upset me," Mr. Dunblane said in a different tone. "You have only made me wonder if what you said was not true. I have been so furious at being smashed up and so angry at being blind that until this moment it did not strike me that it was extraordinary that I was not killed outright."

"I think you were meant to live," Susanna said softly. "Perhaps there is something important and special for you to do in the world, so that you are wanted here. I don't believe that these things ever happen by chance."

"A miracle," Mr. Dunblane muttered to himself.

Then, pushing his shoulders back a little more comfortably against the cushions behind him, he said,

"Very well, I am prepared to listen while you expound your theories. At least they are different and give me something to think about."

"The Secret Doctrine that has been expounded by many leaders," Susanna began –

*

They talked and argued until luncheon time and when she left him Susanna was sure, although he would not admit it, that Mr. Dunblane was tired.

She and Mr. Chambers had just finished their luncheon on the terrace when Clint came to say,

"I've got the Master back to bed, sir. He was quite ready to go and was asleep before I left the room."

"That is good," Mr. Chambers said. "Do you think it wise for me to get in touch with a local doctor? I know that Sir William wrote to one."

"It'd only annoy the Master," Clint replied, "and it'd be best to leave him alone until he's settled down after the journey."

"Very well, we will do what you suggest," Mr. Chambers nodded, "and now Miss Brown and I are going into Florence. We will not be long in case Mr. Dunblane wants us when he awakes."

"You can be certain that's what he'll want," Clint said, "especially Miss Brown."

He gave Susanna what was almost an impudent grin as he added,

"You keep his mind off himself and his injuries, miss, and that's the best medicine anyone of us could give him."

"Thank you," Susanna smiled.

Then she rose to her feet saying to Mr. Chambers,

"I will fetch my hat, it will not take more than a minute."

She was so afraid that they might have to postpone their exploration at the last moment that only when they were driving towards the City could she relax and look round her, excited as a child at everything she saw.

She had read for a long time last night how in the middle-ages Florence was the fashion centre of the world and not only developed woollen goods from raw materials for themselves but sold as many as ten thousand pieces a year to England, Flanders and France.

It would be fun, she thought, to buy some of the silk that Florence was famous for now and also the lace made by the nuns in the Convents and which she knew came from the various hill towns that all had their special designs, each one different from the others.

Then she remembered that she would have to be careful with her money and thought it would be a question of window-shopping rather than being able to acquire the fabrics, some of which she could see hanging up to dry from the windows in the streets that they were passing through.

The colours were striking and she remembered she had read that the colours of Florence were particularly those of the autumn sunset sky, rose and green, golds, scarlet, storm-cloud blue, olive, yellow, ivory and oyster-white.

They drove on, crossing the river. Susanna looked enquiringly at Mr. Chambers and he said,

"I know without your telling me that the one place you want to go to first is the Uffizi Gallery and the rest can wait."

"Thank you, how kind you are."

"As I expect you know," Mr. Chambers replied, "the Uffizi Gallery was created by the Grand Dukes of the house of Medici at the end of the sixteenth century. It was built around the collection begun by Cosimo il Vecchio and his grandson, Lorenzo the Magnificent, enlarged it into the greatest repository of arts in the then known world."

In Florence one always came back, Susanna thought, to Lorenzo and she knew when she stood in front of his terracotta bust that he looked exactly as she had expected.

She had known that he was not outstandingly handsome, not at all like the statues sculpted by Michelangelo, but she had expected that he would look strong, virile and overwhelmingly masculine.

There was a determination in his face that made her feel he would conquer people not only physically but mentally.

She thought too that, if his eyes looked into hers, they would reach deep into her soul and she would find it hard to hide anything from him.

She stood staring at the bust for so long that Mr. Chambers, who had moved away to look at other things, came back to say,

"If you want to see the Botticellis before we return, I think you must leave Lorenzo for the moment."

Susanna gave a little sigh and declared,

"He is really magnificent!"

Then she let Mr. Chambers lead her to the pictures that she had longed to see for so long, only finding herself somewhat sidetracked into feeling that Lorenzo was different from what she had ever felt about anything else.

There was so much to see and everything was so breathtakingly beautiful that it was only when she got back to the Villa that she felt that she must try to express the rapture it all had aroused in her.

Clint was waiting for them saying reproachfully,

"Mr. Dunblane's been awake some time and he's a surprise for you."

"What is it?" Susanna asked.

She pulled off her hat, smoothed down her hair with her hands and hurried to the bedroom.

Clint opened the door and her first glance at the man sitting by the window told her what the surprise was. The bandages had been taken from Mr. Dunblane's arms and now only his head and neck were still encased in them.

She gave a little cry of delight.

"That is better, much better!" she exclaimed. "Now you will be able to feel things with your hands as well as listen to them with your ears."

"I thought what you would say would be appropriate to the occasion," Mr. Dunblane remarked.

As she walked towards him, he said in the dry voice he often used when they argued,

"I suppose you are longing to eulogise over the pictures you have seen. So get it over, since you intend to do so with or without my permission."

"I have so much – to tell you," Susanna answered.

"Most of it will undoubtedly bore me. I will do my best not to yawn, but I may fall asleep."

"That, of course, would be good for you, so I shall not be able to make any complaint!" Susanna retorted.

As she spoke, she looked at his hands and thought that they were very expressive.

It was Miss Harding who had taught her not only to look at people's faces when she appraised them but also their hands.

"Hands can tell you a great deal about a person's character," she had said. "Hands can be coarse or delicate, artistic or common. They can also betray the sensitive instincts of those who may wish to hide them."

Susanna thought now that Mr. Dunblane's hands were strong and well formed.

She thought too that someone who understood such things would think that there was something generous in the long stretch between the thumb and the first finger.

"What are you thinking?" he asked.

"I was looking at your hands."

"Are you trying to judge me by my fingers just as, of course, I can judge you by your voice?"

"I think that is making character study too easy," Susanna argued. "Considering that we are each of us, a complicated whole, to judge one part by itself might give one an entirely wrong impression."

"Are we talking about you or me?"

"Perhaps both."

"Then you would rather I did not assume that, because your voice has a particularly golden quality, the rest of your character equals it."

Susanna drew in her breath trying to think what she could say, but before she could do so, he gave a short laugh,

"I am diverting you from what you want to tell me. Now then, whom do you most closely resemble, Venus or the Lippi Madonna, whose brains have aroused your admiration more than her beautiful face?"

"They were both unbelievably lovely," Susanna answered, "and for the moment it is almost impossible to separate in my mind the wonders I have seen this afternoon in that wonderful, wonderful treasure house."

"Nevertheless I am waiting to hear what you think of Lorenzo the Magnificent."

Susanna started and looked at him in surprise.

"How did you know – I had seen his bust?"

"I was quite certain that you would seek it out because whenever you have talked about him I have known that he interests you perhaps more than any living man has been able to do."

"How could you know – that?" Susanna enquired.

"That is a foolish question because you must be aware that your all-revealing voice told me or perhaps, who knows, I was using my *Third Eye!*"

Susanna was embarrassed that he should realise that she had thought of Lorenzo the Magnificent almost as if he was a real man who was still alive ever since she had read about him on the train.

"I suppose you know," Mr. Dunblane said mockingly, "that Signor Guicciardini, whom you quoted as being an adverse critic, has left on record that he was licentious, very amorous and yet constant in his loves, which usually lasted several years."

"Guicciardini was always finding fault," Susanna replied. "He was quite obviously jealous."

Mr. Dunblane laughed and she realised that he had been deliberately teasing her into a defence of the man she admired.

"I wonder," he said reflectively, "if you met Lorenzo today, if he came to this Villa this afternoon, what you would think of him. Perhaps you would be disappointed. Heroes are often very disillusioning when one meets them in the flesh."

"He must have been like his bust," Susanna said, "and that portrays him as a very strong masculine-looking man."

"Is that what you are looking for in a husband?"

"I have told you that I shall never marry," Susanna answered, "and I have no wish to – talk about it."

"Then you are very different from most women, who not only want to be married but talk about it incessantly!"

"You should be grateful that I am different, sir."

"I find it hard to believe that you should take up such an attitude. Has some man frightened and shocked you or perhaps deserted you, so that you have a dislike of the whole male sex?"

"No! No! It's nothing like that," Susanna cried. "It is just that I know that I shall – never marry."

"Well, that is different. What you were saying before, or rather what I thought you said, was you that had no wish to marry. That is not the same as saying that you will not have the chance."

"Must we talk about me?" Susanna asked. "Why not let me cross-examine you and ask why *you* are not married."

"That is quite an easy question to answer," he replied, "I have never met anyone whom I thought I could tolerate for the rest of my life and, unlike most of my countrymen, I have a firm dislike of the Divorce Courts."

"Then you should live in England," Susanna said, "where divorce, as you know, is considered to be an outrage and very few people will face the ostracism that makes a martyr even of the innocent party."

"If I marry, it will be for ever," Mr. Dunblane stated firmly. "I loathe publicity and have no intention of allowing reporters to pry into my private affairs."

He spoke in a manner that made Susanna think that he had already suffered from that type of interference in the past.

Then she said,

"If you assume that I have found my ideal man in Lorenzo, which picture in Florence depicts your ideal woman?" Mr. Dunblane laughed.

"You are not going to catch me as easily as that! A cleverly baited trap, Miss Brown. But that has always been a feminine perquisite and let me tell you that this conversation is aggressively feminine!"

"You started it!" Susanna flashed.

"But I was being masculine in being interested in you."

"I think it unlikely that you could be anything else."

"Why should you say that ?"

"Because I think that like Lorenzo you are masculine in your desire to dominate everyone and to rule the people around you in a manner that in broader spheres would make you a tyrant!"

She was being deliberately provocative and, as if he knew that it was a challenge, he said,

"Bravo! A clever way of getting out of an uncomfortable position. But let me tell you, Miss Brown, I am now interested in you because it is something you don't want me to be. And, as I cannot read a book, I am forced to read people from what I can only hear and sense."

"I suppose because that is what I urged you to do, I cannot now complain if you carry out my advice, but I would rather you chose someone else."

"I would point out that my choice is limited. I already know all there is to know about Chambers and Clint and, unless I am to concentrate on the servants, that only leaves you."

Susanna rose to stand at the window looking out into the garden.

"I suppose that were you here in other circumstances," she said after a minute, "the Villa would be full of people. There must be many neighbours who would be pleased to see you again."

"If you think I want other people's company, you are mistaken," he answered. "I have no wish for anyone to see me as a figure of fun."

"No one would think that, sir," Susanna said quickly. "They would be sorry, desperately sorry, at what has happened to you, but at the same time they would be glad that you were still alive."

As she spoke, she saw his fingers move in response to what she had said and she thought that now the bandages had been removed she would find it easier to know what he was feeling.

"If you are better tomorrow," she went on, "you will be able to sit in the garden. You will then be able to smell the flowers, hear the hum of the bees and the flutter of birds in the trees."

"I understand that you are telling me what to make myself aware of."

"I cannot believe you are so obtuse that you would not notice it yourself without any help from me."

"I have never employed a reader before," he said, "and I am just wondering to what category a reader belongs."

Susanna did not reply and he carried on,

"You talk to me quite differently from the way that anyone on my staff has ever spoken to me before."

Susanna looked at him apprehensively,

"I am – sorry if I do anything – wrong. I can only excuse myself by saying that this is the first time I have been employed as a reader."

"I am not complaining. I am only saying that it is unusual. What you are doing, Miss Brown, and I think you are doing it deliberately, is to make me think. I am just wondering which of my doctors sent you to me. Could it be one of those psychiatrists whom most Americans find indispensable?"

"It was neither," Susanna answered him. "I saw your advertisement in *The Times* and came round the next morning. I expected when I did so to find the position already filled."

"It was really chance? No one had suggested to you that you ought to help me?"

"No one."

As she spoke, Susanna pondered, as she had done so often, what was happening at Lavenham House. She was well aware that both her mother and her father must have been very angry at her behaviour and she wondered how they were setting about trying to find her.

If they did find her, Susanna thought, then the battle over her marriage would start again. And it would be very difficult for her to escape a second time.

She felt herself shiver at the thought and Mr. Dunblane asked,

"What is troubling you?"

"How do you know I am – troubled?"

"I am not going to try to put into words something which you can explain far better than I can."

Susanna gave a little sigh.

"Please stop being perceptive about me, sir. When I tried to help you by telling you about your *Third Eye*, I did not want it directed towards me."

"You are hiding something from me and perhaps everyone else," Mr. Dunblane said. "What have you done? Committed a murder?"

Susanna laughed as if she could not help it.

"No, not as bad as that."

"But you are hiding from something or perhaps somebody?"

"Why must you ask me so many questions?"

"Because I have little else to do and also, if you want the truth, you interest me."

"Let's be interested in something else. There is so much else to talk about."

"If you are referring to the pictures, I am sick to death of them," he asserted positively. "The women depicted on canvas have all been dead for centuries, you are alive, very much alive, and owing as you say to a miracle, I am alive too! Let's concentrate on that."

His voice seemed to vibrate between them and Susanna said,

"Let me tell you – that if you – become interested in me, just because there is no one else – eventually you will be disappointed! I am warning you, sir – forget me."

It struck her as she spoke, how unwise she had been not to tell him how unattractive and plain she was when they had first met.

Instead she had deliberately allowed him to think that she might look like Lippi's Madonna and now it was too late to retract.

To explain that she was just a fat plain girl whom no man would look at twice, unless he wanted her money, was impossible.

She looked out at the flowers, exquisite in the sunshine and found herself asking in her heart with a kind of agony, why she could not have been like them.

'Mama is so beautiful. Papa is so handsome. May is lovely. Oh God, why am I the exception?'

As she spoke the words silently in her mind, she felt that her feelings were the same as Mr. Dunblane's when he cried out against the darkness in which he could not see.

'The cross he has to bear,' Susanna thought, 'may only be for a very short while, but mine is with me for life.'

"Come here," Mr. Dunblane said suddenly, his voice breaking in on her thoughts.

She turned obediently and walked towards him.

"Give me your hand," he added and held out his.

Because he asked it of her, Susanna laid her fingers on his palm.

"Now tell me what is upsetting you," he demanded gently. "I can feel it vibrating from you almost as if, like me, you are in pain."

Her fingers fluttered in his, but he would not release them.

"Tell me," he insisted.

She felt as if he was overpowering her and forcing her to do what he wanted until with a little cry she snatched her hand away.

"You are – hypnotising me and I am – frightened."

She moved away from him to stand once again at the window and she knew without looking back that his hand lay open on the rug that covered his knees.

She was not only frightened of what he had said but also by what she felt when he touched her.

It was a feeling that she had never known before.

She had thought that she felt helpless and dominated by someone stronger than herself, and there had been another feeling too, which she could neither analyse nor have any wish to do so.

"There is something I want to say – " he began, but at that moment the door opened and Clint appeared with a tray.

"What is it?" Mr. Dunblane enquired.

"I have brought your tea, sir, and Mr. Chambers is waiting on the terrace for Miss Brown."

"I will – go to him at – once," Susanna stammered.

She thought as she spoke that her voice sounded rather strange and she was certainly glad to escape.

*

Late that night Susanna could not sleep. She had twisted and turned, throwing herself about in the comfortable bed in the beautiful room that she had felt an atmosphere of sanctity in until it had become mingled with her own thoughts and feelings.

It was also very hot.

"Unprecedentedly so for March," Mr. Chambers had said earlier.

"It can often be very hot here in April," he went on, "and the doctors insisted that Mr. Dunblane must go to a warm climate, so I am grateful even though I personally find the heat oppressive."

"I like it," Susanna had said, feeling as if the sunshine warmed her heart.

But now tonight she had felt as if there was not enough air to breathe.

She guessed that it must be after two o'clock in the morning and thought that far away in the distance she had heard one of the many Churches in Florence strike the hour.

'I cannot sleep because I am being foolish about Mr. Dunblane,' she told herself severely.

But nevertheless she had found herself going over their conversation again and again and feeling as if he was confused in her mind with Lorenzo the Magnificent.

'When the bandages are removed, what will he look like?' she wondered. 'The man who had ruled Florence over four centuries ago?'

She laughed at herself for being so imaginative. In all probability Mr. Dunblane was an ordinary unattractive American and she would be very stupid to have imaginative ideas about him.

Yet because he and the bust of Lorenzo kept on haunting her she climbed out of bed and walked to the window.

She pulled back the curtains and found that the world outside was even more beautiful than it had been before darkness fell.

Now the moon was out, glinting on the domes and steeples in the City, the sky was full of brilliant stars and below her Susanna could see the river silver as it flowed beneath the bridges.

The garden was full of mysterious dark shadows and yet it was easy to discern the cypress trees and the patches of white where the lilies grew.

The window was open and on an impulse Susanna put on her dressing gown and, slipping her feet into soft-soled slippers, walked across the verandah onto the grass beyond.

The air was warm and heavy and, as she moved towards the flowers, there was the fragrance of night-scented stock that seemed to envelop her as if it was part of a dream.

She walked on and then suddenly came upon a mirror, which reflected the light from the sky and the fireflies floating above it and realised that it was the swimming pool.

Then she drew in her breath with the wonder of it because the air was filled with myriads of flickering fireflies.

Their sparkling beauty was like the galaxy of the Milky Way overhead and intermingled with the lights of Florence below.

Susanna knew at once that she was in Fairyland.

It had a romantic enchantment that had not been there in the day and Susanna thought that her feet had deliberately carried her here so that she could bathe secretly and alone in the quietness of the night.

The only person who might have been about was Mr. Chambers, but he had told her when she said 'goodnight' to him that he was very tired.

"I have not been sleeping well recently," he said, "but I have a feeling that tonight I shall sleep for the prescribed eight hours."

"I am sorry if I have made you do too much today."

"That was a pleasure," he replied, "but there have been problems with Mr. Dunblane's business affairs which have, I admit, taken their toll of me these last few weeks."

He obviously did not wish to say anything more and Susanna wondered again apprehensively if Mr. Dunblane was in financial trouble.

Now she decided, with Mr. Chambers fast asleep and the servants all in a very different part of the Villa, that there would be no one to know what she did.

She remembered that there were bathing dresses in the little pavilion at the end of the swimming pool, but, daringly she did something that she had never done in her life before – she decided to bathe naked.

'I will pretend I am one of the Goddesses who are depicted beautifully in the Gallery,' she thought, 'even Venus herself, not rising from the waves, but walking down into the water with the light of the moon and the glitter of stars to guide her!'

Her imagination captured the idea and she was no longer plain fat Susanna, but Venus, perfectly proportioned with a body as lovely as her face and her golden hair hanging over her white shoulders.

Slowly, without hurrying, Susanna moved into the shallow part of the pool.

Then, as the water rose higher and higher, she struck out swimming as she had done when she was a child, her arms and legs moving rhythmically without undue effort.

"You look like small tadpoles," her father had laughed when she and May had swum in their lake.

But now Susanna knew that she was not animal or human, but Divine!

The Goddess of Love, who could raise men's hearts so that they sought the rapture that only she could bring them and knew that without it their lives would be empty and desolate.

The water was warm and soft as milk as Susanna swam up and down the pool for a long time.

When finally she climbed up the steps and walked across the grass, she raised her arms towards the sky. It was an expression of worship and also one of wonder.

For a short while she had forgotten herself, while the water and the moonlight had swept her into an ecstasy in which she was part of all beauty and was herself beautiful.

Because she was still Venus, a longing within her that she had never expressed before came to her lips,

'Give me – *love*!'

The words were only a whisper and yet she felt that they were carried up into the sky by a force that she had no control over.

# CHAPTER FIVE

Driving back from Florence in the carriage beside Mr. Chambers, Susanna held a parcel tenderly in her hands.

She had spent a long time in the shops on the Ponte Vecchio buying a present for Mr. Dunblane.

Finally, after a great deal of deliberation, she had chosen an eighteenth century musical box which played a gay little tune that the shopkeeper told her, the pheasants had danced to in Medieval times.

Now, knowing what she was thinking Mr. Chambers said,

"I am sure that Fyfe will be delighted with your present. He has no family to remember him on special occasions."

"His father and mother are dead, I understand."

"Yes, and he has always been a very lonely person despite – "

Mr. Chambers stopped and did not finish the sentence.

"I am so glad you told me that it was his birthday today," Susanna said. "I would never have known it otherwise."

"I should really be giving you a present."

Susanna looked at Mr. Chambers in surprise and he explained,

"I cannot tell you what a difference your being here has made not only to my employer but also to me."

"I – don't think – I understand."

"When we crossed the Atlantic after his accident," Mr. Chambers said, "I thought that I would never be able stand the tension of living with him in such circumstances."

He smiled at her as he added,

"I have known Fyfe ever since he was a boy and been in the position not only of secretary, but what Royalty would call a Comptroller. Yet when after his accident he was in despair about his eyesight, I felt helpless and as much of a stranger to him as if I had never known him before."

"It must have been very difficult for you," Susanna smiled sympathetically.

"It was," Mr. Chambers agreed. "Then you arrived and everything was different."

"It is sweet of you to say that."

"I mean it. You have not only helped him through what must be the most difficult time in his life but also given him new horizons of the mind."

Mr. Chambers laughed.

"I feel that am sounding quite poetic, but there is no other way to express how you have introduced him to new subjects and, I think, made him use his brain in a way that he has never used it before."

"It is wonderful to hear you say such things!" Susanna cried. "And I have never been so happy in the whole of my life."

"You look happy," he agreed, "your whole being vibrates with it."

"It is very exciting when we are discussing the books I read aloud."

"There was a thrill in Susanna's tone as if she was speaking to herself and then she added anxiously,

"I do hope that the books we ordered from Paris – will have arrived."

"I am sure they will," Mr. Chambers replied reassuringly.

"It is a very long list. We have both become so interested in the works of Gustave Flaubert."

"I have heard you arguing about *Education Sentimentale*, Mr. Chambers remarked, "and I wondered if *Madame Bovary* was suitable literature for a young lady like yourself."

"I think when we are arguing that Mr. Dunblane and I think of each other as literary critics!"

She made a little sound which was one of delight remembering how they had duelled over Gautier's *Einaux et Camées*, Mr. Dunblane thinking it the work of a craftsman, while she had found it lyrical and romantic.

Perhaps, Susanna thought to herself, the books she read in French were more exciting than those they had chosen in English and Italian.

Yet she knew if she was honest that it was not the books that mattered, but the man who was listening.

A man who was ready to confront her the moment she ceased reading with erudite questions which she delighted to answer while thinking out others to confound him with.

The only difficulty was that like many other teachers she found it hard to keep ahead of her pupil.

Only by reading late at night after she had gone to bed and reading every second she was not actually in his company, could she feel that she had something new to talk to him about and some fresh twist of phrase.

"As I was saying," Mr. Chambers continued, "because you have been so helpful, indeed I think 'wonderful' is the right word, the disease that I was told I had contracted no longer menaces me."

"You mean – your diabetes is cured?" Susanna enquired.

"Almost completely. I was examined by the doctor yesterday whom Sir William recommended when we were in England both for Mr. Dunblane and myself and he has given me a practically clean bill of health!"

Susanna gave a little cry of delight.

"Oh, I am so glad. I knew that you were feeling ill when we arrived here and indeed you looked very tired and worried."

"I was both," Mr. Chambers admitted, "but now, thanks to you rather than the doctor's medicine, I am a different man."

*

The day after they had arrived at the Villa he had said to Susanna,

"I am afraid. Miss Brown, I have to keep to a very strict diet prescribed by my doctor in America. He suspected, which has been confirmed by a specialist in England, that I have a touch of diabetes."

"That means sugar in the blood, does it not?" Susanna asked.

Mr. Chambers nodded his head and explained,

"I am therefore not allowed to eat anything sweet or in fact anything that has sugar in it. The chef understands this and, of course, he will provide you with any dishes you particularly like. You have only to tell him your preferences."

Susanna had at first been too concerned with Mr. Dunblane to really think about what she ate and then she found that the food at the Villa was so delicious that she had no wish to make any changes.

They had *fritto misto mare*, which all Italians enjoy, followed by delicious dishes of very tender veal, kids boiled in white wine, ducks and geese stuffed with quinces and garlic, which were all traditional specialties of Florence.

There were fresh vegetables from the garden and fruit, which grew more profusely as the weather became hotter and spring began to turn into summer.

Small red *fraises des bois* appeared on the breakfast table and there were cherries, apricots and greengages, which Susanna could see ripening on the trees in the orchard.

Most of the time she was so intent on talking to Mr. Chambers about their joint interest, which was Mr. Dunblane, that she had little time to consider what she was eating.

Perhaps because they were isolated in a small world of their own they had all grown very close and friendly towards each other.

It was Mr. Dunblane who had said to Susanna firmly on about the third day they were in Florence,

"I absolutely refuse to go on calling you 'Miss Brown', which I am certain is not your real name."

"Why should you be – certain of that?" Susanna countered just to be argumentative.

"You don't sound like a Miss Brown," he replied, "and I don't think that Susanna is a suitable name for you either."

"It is the only one I have," Susanna replied. "It was chosen for me by my Godmother."

She wondered what he would say if she added,

' – who left me a large fortune.'

"Then 'Susanna' it will have to be," he said with a sigh, "and I hope you will call me 'Fyfe'."

"Surely it is very unconventional for an employee to address her employer in such a familiar manner?" Susanna teased.

"I have already said that you are a very unusual employee," he replied. "In fact I often feel that *you* are giving the orders and *I* am obeying them!"

Susanna gave a little laugh.

She was quite certain that like Lorenzo the Magnificent he would always be the Ruler and the Commander in life.

At first she had felt shy of calling him by his Christian name, but after a while she grew used to it.

Because he always called his secretary 'Chambers', there was no question that Susanna would address him except as Mr. Chambers, but, as if he thought that such respect was due only to his age, he called her by her Christian name.

"Do you realise," Susanna said now as the horses began to climb up the hill towards the Villa, "we have been here for nearly a month? Sometimes it seems as if the weeks have passed in a matter of seconds, at others as if I had lived here always and known no other life."

"Time is relative," Mr. Chambers answered. "When one is happy, it passes in a flash, when one is worried or miserable, it drags its feet in an infuriating manner."

Susanna did not reply.

She was thinking with a kind of horror that her days were numbered.

When the bandages were finally removed from Fyfe's eyes, he would not only no longer need her, but she knew that anyway she must leave.

She could not bear that he should see what she really looked like, when he was still thinking that she was beautiful and resembled the pictures in the Uffizi Gallery.

Only yesterday he had remarked, *à propos* of nothing,

"I was thinking I would like to see you painted in the garden. And, of course, the right setting would be with the lilies all around you."

Susanna drew in her breath.

She had described to him so often how beautiful the lilies looked growing in a profusion that she had never seen before.

They made one corner of the garden where they were framed by green shrubs and cypress trees a picture of such beauty that she felt she must pray every time she saw it.

"Perhaps you would look best in that alcove in the sitting room," Fyfe had gone on reflectively. "It would make you seem as if you were in a shrine.

Susanna had risen hastily to her feet.

"You are being too imaginative," she said. "Anyway, I have no wish to be painted."

"Why not?" Fyfe asked. "Surely those who love you would want to remember you as you look now? Like a rose coming into bud."

"You are quoting from that ridiculous book we read yesterday," Susanna countered crossly. "I am not in the least like a rose."

"At the moment you certainly sound like a flower that has plenty of thorns," Fyfe retorted.

"Mind they don't prick you!" Susanna snapped.

Then they laughed like two children who found the game they were playing irresistibly amusing.

"I have told you before not to talk about me," Susanna said reseating herself, "and just as a punishment I am going to read you an extremely dull article on the world situation!"

"If you do, I shall throw something at you," Fyfe threatened. "And blind or not I would not mind taking a bet that I shall hit you!"

"In which case I shall certainly throw something back," Susanna replied, "and I have the advantage that I shall be able to see where I am aiming."

"That will make no difference since, as you are a woman, you will undoubtedly miss me."

They sparred with each other in a way that would have delighted Mr. Chambers.

Fyfe was no longer sensitive about speaking of his injuries. He never talked of being blind for life, but was optimistically making plans as to what he would do as soon as the bandages were removed.

Susanna, however, wanted to change the conversation to other subjects.

She shrank away from visualising what would happen when she could no longer stay with him, when he would go back to the life he had known before and be surrounded by his friends.

Sometimes she read about them in the newspapers and he would make disparaging comments.

"They always describe Loraine as 'the most beautiful girl in America'," he said once, "but I can tell you she has the temper of the Devil and, once she gets her claws into some wretched man, she squeezes him dry!"

As she spoke, Susanna was glad that the girl, whose face she was looking at in the magazine, did not attract him.

She found herself unaccountably jealous when he spoke about the past with pleasure.

"Dear old Chris. I am glad he is getting married at last!" he said of some notable young Senator. "But I suppose that will mean goodbye to his bachelor parties. God, they were fun! No one ever went home until the dawn broke."

Susanna had not replied and after a moment he said,

"I suppose you have never been to an American party?"

"Or to any – other sort of party," Susanna replied truthfully.

"Why not?"

She was just about to say that she had not been allowed to, when she remembered that she was pretending to be older than she really was.

She kept silent and after a moment Fyfe said,

"I assume that your parents could not afford parties. When I am well, we will give a party that is more original and different from anything anyone has given before."

He thought for a moment and then he continued,

"Everything will be ablaze with lights because I can see them. The house, the garden and the flowers will be lit and there will be fireworks lighting up the sky."

"They will not be as effective as the stars or the fireflies," Susanna pointed out.

She thought how every night when she slipped out to swim in the pool the fireflies seemed to envelop her as if they were the children of the stars.

It was then she imagined to herself that they were part of the light that emanated from her because she really was the Goddess she pretended to be.

She had never quite captured the ecstasy of that first night when she had thought of herself as Venus and became one with the wonder and beauty of the whole Universe.

It was nevertheless an enchantment that never palled to swim naked in the warm water, to smell the fragrance of the garden all around her and to feel that Heaven itself blessed her.

"What are you thinking about?" Fyfe asked her suddenly.

"I was wondering how soon you will be able to swim in that beautiful pool that your father built."

"Very soon," he replied. "I have no bandages left on my arms now, the skin has healed completely."

"I am – so glad."

"Clint tells me that there are a few scars left. I suppose I shall have those for the rest of my life, but as I am not a woman it will not matter. Is your skin white?"

His question made Susanna start. She put out her arm as if she inspected it for the first time.

"I suppose it must have been before I came here," she replied, "but as I walk about the garden without a hat and without a sunshade it now has a touch of gold."

"Like your voice."

There was something in the way he spoke which sent a little thrill through her.

Last night, when she had crept out into the garden to bathe in the pool, she had sat on the edge of it and looked up at the sky.

There was no moon, but the stars were so brilliant that it was possible to see clearly. The fireflies were dancing above their reflection in the water.

'The first night I came here,' Susanna told herself, 'I asked God to give me love. He has answered my prayer, but it is more of an agony than a joy.'

She had faced the fact a long time ago that she loved Fyfe in a way that she had never thought it possible to love anybody.

It was a blessing and a delight to be with him.

It was an agony that was physical as well as mental to know that she could never mean anything in his life and that she would have to spend the future without him.

She was far too intelligent to think that her Fairy story could end happily or that Prince Charming would ever care for her as she cared for him.

She knew only too well what he would think when he first saw her.

'I love him!' Susanna said to the stars, 'and I must never regret that I have known love and that it can fill my life as it does now to the exclusion of all else. But this is only a dream.'

She went on to think that it was a dream so beautiful and so perfect that she should go down on her knees in gratitude that she had been given what she had asked for and it was even more wonderful than she had imagined it could ever be.

But the awakening drew nearer every day.

Then there would be the loneliness and the thought of the long years ahead when Fyfe would not be there and she would only have her memories of him.

Because she knew that every minute and every second was precious, she was always with him unless he was asleep.

In consequence she had seen little of Florence, simply because even to look at the buildings, the pictures and the sculptures was a waste of time if she could be with Fyfe instead.

Because she was in love she wanted to make him happy.

She had found not only a large library in the Villa that was filled with books collected by his father, mostly about Italy, but Mr. Chambers had only too willingly agreed to send to Rome and Paris for other books that she felt would interest not only Fyfe but herself.

She blessed Miss Harding who had opened her eyes to so many literary giants who she would otherwise never have heard of.

Miss Harding's father had been a teacher of literature at one of the famous Public Schools and her knowledge ranged over so many different fields that Susanna now found stood her in good stead.

"I think French is more suited to your voice than any other language," Fyfe had said after she had read to him *Les Fleurs du Mai* by Charles Baudelaire.

Again it was a strange choice, although she was not aware of it, for a young girl.

Baudelaire drew poetry from reality. He was haunted by a sense of damnation, which drove him to revolt and blasphemy.

He longed for the discovery of the Beyond and his poems gave rise to arguments on the After Life, which had

Susanna and Fyfe sparring with each other until Clint insisted that his patient should go to bed.

"I refuse to be bullied," Fyfe said angrily. "For Heaven's sake stop croaking at me!"

"You know what the doctor said, sir," Clint retorted. "'Rest, rest, rest!' That's one thing your tongue's not doin' nor your mind."

"If I want to stay up, I shall do so," Fyfe thundered.

Susanna had risen to her feet.

"Clint is right," she said. "We can go on discussing this tomorrow and doubtless in the quiet watches of the night I shall think up some further ammunition to fire at you."

"And doubtless look up some sources for it," Fyfe responded. "It's not fair. I am going to think of a way that you can be handicapped so that occasionally I can win the race."

"Perhaps I will be magnanimous and let you win one occasionally," Susanna replied.

She had left his bedroom as he shouted after her that he wanted no favours.

She had been laughing as she went into her own room. Then she had undressed and sat up in bed reading, until it was late enough for her to go into the garden and swim.

*

The horses had reached the Villa and Susanna looked for the first glimpse of the long white building between the cypress trees.

'It is like reaching Paradise to be home,' she thought to herself.

But she knew that it was not the Villa that drew her, but the man it contained.

There was a short drive, then as Susanna had her first glimpse of the front door, she drew in her breath.

There were a number of men outside it, all talking it seemed at once.

"Who are – they? What do they – want?" she asked Mr. Chambers hesitantly and she saw the frown between his eyes.

The horses drew to a standstill and the men, eight of them, turned with an expression of interest, to look at the new arrivals.

Susanna saw Clint standing in the doorway and realised that he had been talking to the men. There was something in his attitude that told her without words that he was on the defensive.

Susanna climbed out of the carriage carrying her present carefully and, as Mr. Chambers followed, one of the men asked,

"Are you Mr. Falcon's secretary ?"

"If I am, what has that to do with you?" Mr. Chambers asked.

"I represent the *New York Herald*," the man replied. "We've been trying to find out where Mr. Falcon had gone and now I and these other gentlemen who represent a number of different newspapers are anxious to have a statement from him on the new development of his car."

Mr. Chambers walked up the steps leading into the house before he turned to say,

"Mr. Falcon, as you all know, has had a very serious accident. He has nothing to say at the moment and on his doctor's advice can give no interviews."

As he finished speaking, Mr. Chambers took Susanna by the arm and led her into the Villa.

A roar of questions followed them, some Susanna noted, in English, others in Italian, French and German.

Then the American from the *New York Herald* who had spoken first shouted,

"And who is the pretty dame?"

By this time they were inside the Villa and Susanna thought that the reporter was being sarcastic.

Clint closed the door behind them.

"I'm glad you arrived when you did, sir," he said. "They were so persistent I was afraid they'd force their way in and insist on seein' the Master."

"You know how much he would dislike that," Mr. Chambers replied.

"And yet it wouldn't have been as bad today as it would have been other days," Clint remarked.

Susanna wondered why he should say that.

They were walking along the passage and she realised that Mr. Chambers was going straight to Fyfe's room.

Clint moved ahead to open the door for them and, as if he was determined to have his say first, he announced before either of them could speak,

"Mr. Chambers got rid of them, sir, but they were awful persistent."

As she entered the room, Susanna looked at Fyfe who, as she expected, was sitting in an armchair by the open window.

Then she gave a little cry of surprise and excitement.

His eyes were still bandaged, but it was only a straight bandage encircling his head and all the previous ones that had given him a strange mummified appearance ever since she had first seen him had gone!

His chin, the lower part of his cheeks, half his nose and his neck were clear.

Now he looked really like a man.

Forgetting everything else she ran across the room to kneel down beside his chair to ask,

"Why did you not – tell me? How could I have – guessed that this was – going to happen today?"

"I wanted it to be a surprise," Fyfe answered in his deep voice.

"It is wonderful! Really wonderful! And there are no scars on your face such as you expected."

"That is what Clint said, but are you sure?"

"Completely sure," Susanna answered, looking at the smoothness of his chin.

"It feels tender now that my beard has been shaved off," Fyfe said, putting up his hand, "but I certainly feel more human and no longer a disembodied spirit."

"You were never that," Susanna said, "but it is amazing!"

His skin looked slightly pink, but otherwise there was nothing to show where he had been burnt.

Now, she thought, the only question was whether the operation had been successful and his eyes had been saved.

She did not say so aloud because already Mr. Chambers was talking to him about the reporters.

"They want you to make a statement on the tests of the new model."

"We hardly know anything ourselves yet."

"I said you had no comment to make."

"Cable Stevens is to issue a report as soon as it is available."

"I think it best for you to do that yourself," Mr. Chambers said. "They claimed that there are still adjustments to be made, so let the Press wait for them."

"Yes, you are right," Fyfe agreed. "If they think there is anything new, we shall just have them back again tomorrow."

"I am afraid so," Mr. Chambers agreed. "I suppose it was impossible to cover our tracks completely."

"I am only surprised that they did not find us before," Fyfe said. "You know how persistent they can be once they are on the scent of a story."

"Perhaps we have been fortunate," Mr. Chambers said, "and may I say how glad I am that you are taking it in such a philosophical manner?"

"Perhaps I have acquired some wisdom here in the City of the wise," Fyfe replied, "or perhaps Susanna has taught me a little sense."

"Personally I think the latter is the best explanation," Mr. Chambers said lightly and he walked from the room followed by Clint.

Susanna was still kneeling by Fyfe's chair.

"I am bewildered and curious," she said. "I thought your name was 'Dunblane'."

"It was my mother's and I thought that I was entitled to it when I wished to be incognito."

"So you are really Fyfe Falcon and I must have heard about you if you own the Falcon motor car."

Fyfe put back his head and laughed.

"Such is fame! I always believed myself to be an international figure."

"Well, at least you can have the pleasure of telling me how important you are."

She gave a little cry.

"But of course! You must have raced your own cars. Or were you one of those who recorded such amazing speeds on Daytona Beach?"

"Got it in one!" Fyfe exclaimed. "I always thought you were intelligent, even when it came to motor cars!"

"I admit I know nothing about them," Susanna replied. "Papa has always talked about buying one, but really I preferred his horses. Mama uses an electric brougham sometimes, but I think she feels more elegant when she is driving behind a very smart pair of horses."

"That is sacrilege!" Fyfe exclaimed. "Now that the cat is out of the bag, you are going to have to listen to me eulogising about Falcon cars and if you are bored you can just blame it on the Press who have ferreted me out."

"Have you produced a new car that is very exceptional? Susanna enquired.

"It is a six-cylinder 72 h.p. model," Fyfe replied, "and I am going to enter it for the race next year from New York to Paris. And drive it myself."

"From New York to Paris?" Susanna echoed. "But how? How can you do that?"

"Via Seattle, Japan and Siberia," Fyfe answered. "About twelve thousand miles and I reckon I shall be able to do it in one hundred and seventy days."

"But how can you attempt such a feat? Surely it would be dreadfully dangerous?"

There was a little throb in her voice that made Fyfe reach out his hand to find hers.

"I thought when I left New York more dead than alive," he said, "and was brought to London because they told me that only the London surgeons could save my sight, that I had not a chance in hell of ever seeing again. Now I know that I shall not only see, but I shall drive my new car, as I intended to do."

"How can you be so – sure ?" Susanna whispered.

She could feel herself quiver with strange sensations running through her because he was touching her hand.

"You have made me sure," he answered. "Have you not poured hope and optimism into me in one way or another ever since we came here? You can hardly tell me now that we are on the last lap, that you don't believe I shall win through."

"Yes, of course you will," Susanna whispered.

Then, as if she could not bear to think of it, she said,

"Were you worried and upset the first day we came here when I read to you about Henry Ford's model since you feared that his cars might be more successful than yours?"

"It was a shock to find out that he was competing with my cars," Fyfe replied. "Now I know more, I realise we are not vying with each other in the same market. And I have learned from confidential sources that Ford intends by increased production to reduce his prices every year."

"And that will hurt you?" Susanna queried.

"I don't think so. I am building a much higher quality car, one that you will be proud to be seen in."

His words brought back forcefully to Susanna the thought that, when he could see her, he would be anything but proud for her to be seen in his car.

She rose to her feet saying,

"The reporters made me forget that this is a very special day. Many Happy Returns, Fyfe, and I have a present for you."

She put the parcel she had been carrying in her left hand onto his lap.

"How did you know it was my birthday?" he asked. "I suppose Chambers told you."

"He told me you were twenty-six."

"Almost middle-aged! So I hope you will treat me with respect. But there was no need for you to buy me a present."

"I hope – you will – like it."

He was undoing the wrapping paper carefully and when he had done so he said,

"It's a box and I have the idea that it is painted."

"Open it," Susanna urged him.

He felt with his fingers for the catch and, as he opened the pretty painted lid, the tune began to play and he gave an exclamation of delight.

Susanna was watching the smile on his lips and she thought as she did so that he was in fact even more like Lorenzo the Magnificent than she had really expected him to be.

There was the same firm chin, the same mouth that could be determined, perhaps obstinate, and yet the lips had something sensual about them.

At the thought she drew in her breath knowing that, just as women had pursued Lorenzo and found him attractive, women would also pursue Fyfe.

Much of his nose was still hidden behind the bandage, but his hair was dark and, although it was still very short because it had been scorched by fire, she could see that it waved back from a square forehead.

She was sure that when she could see him completely he would in some ways be more American, and yet undoubtedly there was some resemblance to the terracotta bust of Lorenzo.

As if he sensed her scrutiny, Fyfe asked,

"What are you thinking?"

"If I told you, it might make you conceited!"

"I doubt it. I have the feeling that you are comparing me to Lorenzo the Magnificent and not particularly to my advantage."

Susanna was not really surprised that he should be so intuitive where her thoughts were concerned.

In the last weeks he had, as if on her instructions, trained his *Third Eye* to perceive so much and so acutely that sometimes she forgot that he was blind.

The tune from the little box tinkled to an end.

"It's a lovely present!" Fyfe enthused, "and it was very sweet of you, Susanna, to give it to me. I don't have to tell you that I shall always treasure it."

She wanted to ask him if when she had left him, he would sometimes play it and think of her and then she knew it would be a stupid request.

Once this dream world had come to an end he would go back to a very different one, to his cars, to his racing and to the battle with his competitors not only in a race but for the patronage of the public.

How could he then be expected to remember the woman who had only been a voice in the darkness?

'I have to be practical and use my common sense,' Susanna told herself, 'and that means facing the fact that I shall never, once he can see, mean anything to him – but a memory.'

It was a depressing thought, but she decided she would not let it spoil another precious moment that she could be with him.

"I have so much to tell you about the Ponte Vecchio," she began. "I have never had time before to look in the shops and they are absolutely thrilling! There are so many things made by the Florentine craftsmen that I am quite certain have no equal anywhere else in the world."

"That is what I have always thought," Fyfe said. "As soon as I can see, I want to buy you a piece of jewellery, Susanna, that will not only express my thanks for what you have done for me but be a compliment to your beauty."

His words brought a pain that made Susanna close her eyes for a moment.

Why had she not told him the truth at the very beginning she asked herself for the thousandth time?

How could she have pretended to be what she was not and now know that soon he must face the revelation not only of her appearance but of her duplicity in lying?

She was relieved from saying anything, however, when Clint came into the room carrying a jug of fruit juice which had, now the weather had grown so hot, supplanted the tea that Susanna had been provided with when she first came to the Villa.

Setting the jug down on a table on the verandah, Clint poured out two glasses and handed them on a tray first to Susanna and then to Fyfe.

"What does this contain?" Fyfe asked.

Before Clint could reply Susanna gave a little cry.

"That is cheating! You know you have to guess."

"You are still giving me lessons?" he enquired with a smile.

She thought that she had never seen anything so fascinating as the movement of his lips.

"Of course," she answered. "Even when the last bandage is off you may find it useful to see in the dark like a cat and to know what you are eating and drinking by using your senses correctly."

"Very well, Teacher. I will listen to you for a little while longer," Fyfe replied.

He took a sip from his glass and said,

"This is a juice we have not had before. I thought that we must have tried them all by now."

"Guess!" Susanna insisted.

"I know. Peaches."

Susanna glanced at Clint.

"That's right, sir. The first peaches from the garden came in today and seeing what a good crop we've got I expect you'll have to put up with them now for every meal."

He went from the room as he spoke and Susanna laughed.

"There is always a slight sting in everything Clint says," she commented, "but perhaps that is what makes him so original."

"I am very lucky to have him," Fyfe said. "I know that as I am lucky to have Chambers and of course you, Susanna."

"Have I been – lucky for you?"

"Now you are fishing for compliments!"

He paused for a minute before he said,

"I am saving them all up, as it happens, until I am myself again."

He put his hand to his chin as he went on,

"You don't know what it is like to have those hot restricting bandages removed. Sometimes I felt suffocated by them and I wanted to tear them off."

"That would have been a terrible thing to do."

"Yes, I know. The doctors made it very clear that it would be fatal for them to be taken away before the skin had completely healed."

"And now – as you say – you are nearly yourself."

She thought as she looked at him that he was, as far as she was concerned, different, very different from what he had been before.

Because she was so used to seeing a huge white bandaged mummified head in front of her, she had almost ceased to believe that he could be any different.

But now he was very much an attractive man, a man who made her feel shy when she had not felt shy before, a man she vibrated to in a different way from how she had reacted previously.

"Yes, soon I shall be myself," Fyfe said as if he was following a train of thought, "and yet I almost shrink from stepping back into the world again. Being here in the darkness has been like living on an island in the middle of the Pacific."

It was what Susanna had thought, but she knew that it could never mean to him what it had meant to her.

'I love him!' she told herself, 'but he must never be aware of it because I could not bear his pity any more than I could bear to watch the shock in his eyes when he sees me and realises what I really look like.'

As if the thought was almost too hard to be borne, she put down the glass and said,

"I am going to find out if the books have arrived from Paris. Remember the long list we made? At least some of them should arrive today, but I cannot wait to see if the Gustave Flauberts we asked for are here."

Fyfe did not answer and after a moment she said, a little hesitatingly,

"But perhaps now I know who you are and you no longer have to pretend, you would rather I read you about motor cars? There surely must be plenty about them in the newspapers and magazines?"

"It's strange," Fyfe replied, "but when you first came here I could think of nothing else. Even though it hurt me to do so, I deliberately did not ask you after that first day to read about what was happening in *The Motoring World*, firstly because Chambers told me that to get so agitated would retard my recovery and secondly it infuriated me not to be in America and know exactly what was happening."

Susanna was listening, but she did not speak and he went on,

"Now I feel that I have a thousand interests that demand my attention and if the whole Falcon Empire has fallen to the ground it will be entirely your fault!"

"Adam always blamed Eve," Susanna added quickly.

Then she blushed because she realised that she was suggesting that she was his Eve, which she had no right to do.

"We will talk about our books and all the questions they arouse in us," Fyfe said firmly. "They belong to our island, Susanna, where there are no roads and therefore no place for cars. When we sail away from it, I will tell you and expect you to believe me, that the Falcon is the best and most outstanding car ever designed."

"I reserve the right to question that," Susanna replied. "Being English I naturally think that the Rolls-Royce is the top car of the world, while the French would undoubtedly challenge that statement with their Dion-Bouton."

"Now that is something I *have* to answer – " Fyfe began.

He was exclaiming very volubly on the merits of the Falcon when Mr. Chambers came into the room.

"I have two cables from America," he said, "and I suppose, as Susanna has now been let into the secret of who you are, I can give them to you in her presence."

"Susanna is not the slightest bit interested, so your plan of keeping her in ignorance was quite unnecessary," Fyfe replied. "She had never heard of Fyfe Falcon and wishes only to ride in a Rolls-Royce Silver Ghost!"

Mr. Chambers's eyes were twinkling.

"I can see that this is going to be a real bone of contention. Shall I send for a Falcon car to prove to her its desirability?"

"Certainly not!" Susanna answered before Fyfe could speak. "We have just decided that we are living on an island and therefore the only practical method of leaving it will be by ship."

She went from the room before Fyfe could find words to answer her and, as she walked down the passage, she could hear the two men laughing.

'We are all so happy,' she told herself. 'Oh, please God, don't let him see too quickly.'

Then she was duly horrified at the selfishness of such a prayer.

# CHAPTER SIX

Susanna closed the book with a bang.

"Well, that is finished," she sighed, "and I think for the good of your education we now ought to read something in Italian or English."

"I am not worrying about my education," Fyfe answered, "but my entertainment and I find that English novels are either heavy or too insipid to be interesting and the Italian novels too emotional."

"You might be talking about women." Susanna teased him. "Do you dislike women who are emotional?"

"That is one of those questions that there is no real answer to," Fyfe replied. "If I say 'yes' you will infer that I like cold frigid women who are usually, of course, English and if I say 'no' you will think that I want someone throwing dramatics all the time if they are not being hysterical."

Susanna laughed.

"You must have known some very odd women."

"Perhaps that is true," he agreed.

"And I suppose because you are Fyfe Falcon they flutter around you like moths around a flame."

Because she was being deliberately provocative with such a banal smile, Fyfe groaned and said,

"Of course I want women to applaud my achievements and to tell me I am wonderful. What man wants anything else?"

"Some men must prefer sincerity to flattery."

"I think you will find that all men want to be made a fuss of, which they seldom are."

"That is not true," Susanna argued. "However, you may be speaking as an American and I have always been told that England is a Paradise for men and America for women."

"I wonder what you would think of America?" he remarked reflectively. "It is still basically a new country and in many ways it is very brash. At the same time it is exciting and there is a sense of adventure there that I have not found anywhere else in the world."

The way he spoke made Susanna feel that he was longing to be back in America and she thought with a little stab in her heart that when he did return she would never see him again.

"I love Florence," she said softly.

"Florence, like so much of Europe, lives on the glories of its past. One day it will crumble away and have nothing to show but ruins."

"I will not listen to you!" Susanna said hotly. "There is more beauty in Florence than in the whole of America put together and every stone has a history."

"A history that is all in the past," Fyfe retorted.

She knew that he was deliberately teasing her. Equally she clung to Florence because it was the present and they were together.

She looked out of the window at the brilliant colours of the flowers in the garden and the cypress trees silhouetted against the Madonna blue of the sky.

Below them the dome of the Cathedral seemed to shimmer in the sunshine and the Arno shone as it moved beneath its scores of bridges.

"Could anything be more beautiful?" Susanna asked, almost beneath her breath.

"It's merely a black splodge to me," Fyfe observed.

"Then I will ask you again when they take off your bandages," Susanna said, "and, if you can find a place to compare with it in America, I shall be very surprised."

She could see by his smiling mouth that he was amused by her enthusiasm and after a moment she said in a very different voice,

"When do the doctors plan to – take off your – bandages, Fyfe?"

"I am not certain," he replied. "They have no wish to do anything hastily."

"No – but it must be – soon."

"You sound as if you are impatient to finish your job as a reader."

"No! *No*! Of course not."

The refusal came from her very heart.

He had no idea, she thought, how every morning she awoke thinking that perhaps this day was the last time she would be with him, this would be the day when he would see her face and no longer be interested in her.

Because she was half-afraid that he would sense her agitation, she rose to her feet to stand on the edge of the verandah.

"I am going to pick you some flowers," she said. "It's so hot that those I picked the day before yesterday are already drooping."

"While you are picking flowers," Fyfe said, "tell Chambers to come to me. I want to write a letter to a friend in America."

Although she told herself that she was being ridiculous, Susanna felt a sharp stab of jealousy.

Perhaps he was writing to someone he loved and who, of course, loved him.

What woman would be able to resist him, not only because he was so attractive but also because, she realised now, he was extremely rich?

Fyfe had told her last night how his father had started to manufacture the Falcon car just before he died.

"He already had a huge fortune that he had made in railroads. He was always travel-minded," Fyfe said, "and from the very moment that there was a possibility of a vehicle that could move without horses he had been interested in it."

"When was the first car really invented?" Susanna asked.

"Experiments were going on as early as 1805," Fyfe answered, "but the first cars were really steam-carriages with mechanical legs."

He laughed as he added,

"One of your countrymen, a Dr. Church, had in 1833 an enormous and highly decorated steam-carriage, which accommodated fifty passengers between London and Birmingham."

He smiled as he continued,

"Then, of course, the traditional British caution came into play."

"What do you mean by that?" Susanna asked.

"An Act of Parliament almost killed the development of all horseless carriages by imposing a speed limit of four miles per hour and two miles per hour in towns! They also required that a man should walk sixty yards ahead of every vehicle carrying a red flag."

"Did the Americans take no precautions against such fiery monsters?" Susanna asked.

"We were far more advanced," Fyfe laughed. "Our flagmen had to walk a hundred yards ahead! And our operators were expected to have an engineer's licence, which required several years' apprenticeship as a fireman."

They both laughed and Fyfe went on to tell her how the internal combustion engine was invented, how at the Paris Exhibition in 1865 the Germans showed a free-piston engine and how eventually Daimler and Benz laid the foundations for the development of a successful petrol-engined car.

Susanna found herself becoming more and more excited over the development of the motor car.

She began to appreciate the tremendous battle that the enthusiasts had to fight to make the authorities realise that motor cars had really become a modern form of transport.

"By 1893," Fyfe said, "Benz had a car that was a commercial proposition and was selling quite steadily, especially in France. Daimler formed a Company in Germany to build cars and in America there were factories in Ohio and Pennsylvania.

"My father," he went on, "was determined to build a high quality car and at the same time one which was within the reach of the average businessman's pocket."

"I can now see why," Susanna interposed, "while most schoolboys were content with toy trains, you wanted to play with a real motor car."

"That is true," Fyfe smiled, "I also wanted to see how fast I could go."

"With disastrous results!" she exclaimed. "I hope it has taught you that in future it is better to go slowly and to arrive."

"It has taught me nothing of the sort," he replied. "Like many people you don't understand that for a car to prove itself and to excite the public into buying it, it has to do something sensational."

"But it is dangerous!"

"Only at times. I was just unfortunate. Another time I shall doubtless be more lucky."

She gave a little sigh of exasperation.

"But you cannot be so foolhardy as to go back and – risk your life another time."

"I shall not attempt very high speeds until my eyes are really strong," Fyfe answered, "but there is nothing to stop me from taking part in long endurance races."

"I hate to think of you doing – either."

"Would you really mind if I smashed myself up again?"

It was a question that Susanna knew she dare not answer and she had cleverly changed the subject without his being aware of it, she thought, that she had done so.

Now, as she went to fetch Mr. Chambers to him, she felt as she walked down the cool beautifully furnished corridor of the Villa, that every aspect of it was engraved on her mind for all time.

She knew that in the long years to come she would only have to close her eyes to see, as clearly as if they stood in front of her, every picture, every piece of furniture and every colourful rug that the Villa was furnished with.

But she could not think of Fyfe himself without her heart beating frantically and her love welling up inside her like a tidal wave.

She went into the room that Mr. Chambers used as an office but he was not there.

It was near the front hall and she thought that before she looked for him further that she might see if the postman had left a parcel of books that were still overdue.

The hall was decorated with furniture made by Florentine craftsmen hundreds of years earlier and the walls were decorated with ceramics that were characteristically lovely.

The Florentines were accomplished artists and everything made by them, mirrors, goblets, amphorae, lamps, braziers, had a beauty unsurpassed by those made by any other City in the world.

Beauty was in their blood and it was their tradition.

Susanna had already looked at everything in the hall so that it was imprinted on her mind, but even so every time she saw the ceramics, the statues that guarded the open doors and the gold chandelier hanging from the arched ceiling, she felt herself thrill again at the wonder of them.

The front door was open to let in the sunshine and, as she looked to see if there were any parcels on the carved table where the postman would have left them, she heard the sound of a carriage coming up the drive.

She saw the horses and knew that they were the inferior animals that plied for hire and not the excellent horseflesh behind which she and Mr. Chambers travelled into Florence.

She wondered who could be calling at the Villa and then, as the carriage came nearer, she glanced at the man sitting on the back seat.

He wore a tall hat and was sitting straight and upright, as if he thought that the vehicle he travelled in was not worthy of him.

Susanna's eyes widened and then with a cry of sheer horror she turned and ran back the way she had come.

She pulled open the door of Fyfe's bedroom and rushed across it to where he was sitting in his usual comfortable chair outside the window on the verandah.

By the time she reached him she was breathless, but he sensed her agitation and before she could speak he asked,

"What is the matter? What has upset you?"

"Oh, Fyfe! Fyfe!"

It was a cry that came from her very heart.

Then, as he reached out his hand towards her, she clutched it in both of hers, clinging to it as if it was a lifeline to save her from drowning.

"What is the matter?" Fyfe asked again.

"It's my – father! He has – just arrived – here! He must have – discovered where – I am and has – come to take me away!"

As she spoke, still holding onto Fyfe's hand, she collapsed onto her knees at his side.

"Save – me! *Save – me!*" she pleaded. "If I go – back with him, Mama will – make me marry a man who has no – interest in me – except for my – money."

"Is that why you ran away?"

~143~

"Yes – I could not do it – but they would have – made me. They would have – forced me to – marry and the whole idea was – horrible! Degrading!"

Susanna's voice broke on the words and Fyfe's fingers tightened on hers.

Then he said quietly,

"You say your father has arrived. Did he see you?"

"No. I was in the hall and I – came here at – once to you. Oh, Fyfe – what – can I do?"

It was a cry of despair and with tears now running down her cheeks Susanna stammered,

"If I go – back I am lost – whatever protests I make – no one will listen – to me."

She was sobbing now unrestrainedly, thinking of her mother forcing her to marry the Duke, thinking that she would be looked at with the same disdain and contempt that had been so much a part of her existence before she had come to Florence.

Never had she been able to talk ordinarily and without embarrassment to a man as she had talked to Fyfe and she knew that no other man would want to talk to her in such a way because she was so plain.

She did not know what he could do to save her.

She only turned to him because she loved him and because at the moment he was the only secure and stable thing in her whole life and he filled it to the exclusion of all else.

"Listen, Susanna," Fyfe said quietly, "I want you to go into the garden and hide yourself. Stay away until I send for you. I will deal with this."

"Papa – will insist on – seeing me."

"Leave everything to me. I promise you need not be afraid."

"Papa will be very – angry with me and – Mama will be – furious. How could they have – found me?"

"Just do as I tell you," Fyfe urged, "and go at once. Otherwise if your father insists on seeing you he will find you here."

His words made Susanna jump to her feet like a startled fawn.

Almost as if she could hear her father's footsteps coming down the passage, she looked towards the door apprehensively and then releasing her compulsive hold on Fyfe's hand she slipped away into the garden.

She moved across the lawns and down through the shrubs and bushes until she found a seat concealed by trees and yet with a breathtaking view in front of it.

But for once when she reached the seat, Susanna was not interested in the loveliness that lay beneath her.

Instead she covered her face with her hands and sat wondering desperately how soon it would be before her father forced her to return with him.

She was sure, apart from anything else, that he would be very angry at having to leave London in the middle of the Season to travel to Italy to find her.

She trembled to think what her mother would say when she returned home.

However angry she might be, whatever recriminations and fury descended on her for her behaviour, that would not change one iota the plans that had been made for her future.

If it was not the Duke whom she was to marry, it would be some other Nobleman who would find her fortune attractive enough to put up with her and her shortcomings.

'How can I possibly bear it?' Susanna asked herself.

She knew that since she had known Fyfe and loved him it would be even more difficult and more horrifying to contemplate than before.

For the first time in her life she had been able to talk to someone near her own age as if she was a human being.

Miss Harding had instructed her and given her an insight into knowledge that she would always be grateful for. But Miss Harding had been over fifty and she had at all times been the teacher and Susanna the pupil.

But with Fyfe she had been on equal terms.

When they argued, duelled and sparred with each other and, what was even more important, laughed together, it had been an excitement and an enchantment that she had never known before.

Now it was over, not because Fyfe had no further use for her but because she would be forced to go back to a life that would enclose her like a prison and there would be no escape.

Any man her mother forced her to marry would be part of the frivolous pleasure-seeking Society that Lady Lavenham shone in like a glittering jewel.

The men in that particular Society were concerned only with sport and the women with flirtations and *affaires de coeur*, which occupied their minds to the point where they had no time for anything else.

Susanna knew that, as no one would want to flirt with her, her only asset would be her enormous bank balance.

She would in a short while become nothing but a pale ghost moving from house party to house party or entertaining in the Ducal mansion that had been restored with her money.

She would find herself hostess to people who would not speak to her unless they had to and she would have no interest in anything they did or said because it was in every way alien to her own taste.

'Oh, God,' she prayed, 'save me from that! Make it possible for me to escape again even if I have to live alone and earn my living by going out to – scrub floors.'

But she knew even as she prayed that that too would be an impossibility.

Once she was back with her mother her will would be sapped and she would be married almost before she knew it was happening.

She suspected that the reason why her father had come to fetch her was that her mother had already arranged everything and disliked her plans being circumvented above all else.

'All Mama wants,' Susanna told herself, 'is to get me off her hands and, of course, it will be a feather in her cap for her second daughter to be a Duchess.'

She could hear her sister sobbing, see May's pale unhappy face and felt every nerve in her body tense at the thought of what was waiting for her.

She took her hands from her face and wondered how long she had been sitting on the seat and hiding as Fyfe had told her to do.

Perhaps Clint or one of the other servants was already searching for her to tell her that her father was waiting to take her back to London.

Now she could no longer cry for she was past tears.

She might have known, she thought, that her Fairytale would come to an end or rather that the ship which had come to carry her away from the enchanted island where she had been so happy with Fyfe would be a prison ship.

Once aboard it, a whole train of circumstances that she had no control over would be set in motion.

She wondered if it would be better to die than to endure such a life and then knew that she had not the courage to kill herself nor the means to do it.

'Perhaps I should have drowned myself,' she wondered, 'when I was swimming in the pool last night.'

She had swum, as she always did, up and down for a long time enjoying the exercise as well as the beauty of the stars and the fireflies.

Then she had sat on the steps with her feet in the water thinking of Fyfe and how much she loved him.

Last night she had imagined that he had been Lorenzo the Magnificent in a previous incarnation and she had been the woman he had been faithful to for two years.

To be loved by Fyfe, she told herself, for two years, two months, or even two weeks would be worth all the misery and heartbreak that would follow.

'I love him – *I love him*!' she whispered to the stars, 'and because I asked for love I must never be ungrateful or complain because it hurts me.'

She imagined that she might dare to ask Fyfe before the doctors took the bandages from his eyes to kiss her just once, knowing that he would never wish to do so after he had seen her.

If he kissed her, imagining her to be Venus, then perhaps nothing else after that would matter because she would have her memories.

Even if she went back to England and married the Duke, she told herself, she would still know that her lips had been possessed by Fyfe and she had given him her heart so that it was no longer there in her body to torture her.

Finally, after she had been sitting on the seat for a long time, she knew that what she had imagined under the stars was something that would never happen in reality.

She could not ask Fyfe to kiss her because it would be a betrayal of his trust in her.

'I shall never be kissed by any man,' Susanna thought with a little sob, 'except perhaps by one who is thanking me because, as he does so, he is spending my money! Oh God, if only I could die!'

She said the words aloud and then was ashamed because she knew that it was wicked to take life, which in itself was so precious.

'Perhaps one day there will be some compensation for what I must suffer,' she told herself and wondered what it could possibly be.

Every instinct in her whole body shrank from what her mother had planned for her and yet with all her intelligence she could not think how she could avoid being pressured into marriage or escape again once she had been taken back to London in disgrace.

It suddenly struck her that her father might be rude and disagreeable to Fyfe.

'Perhaps I should have stayed and told Papa that it was not his fault and he had no idea who I was,' she told herself.

Then she thought that, even though his eyes were bandaged and he had nearly lost his life in a motor accident, Fyfe was not the sort of person to be bullied or be afraid of anyone.

Equally it was as if the whole gossamer world that she had encased herself in since coming to Florence had fallen to pieces around her and she looked at it helplessly not knowing how to put it together again.

'Perhaps I should go and pack,' she thought despondently. 'Papa will not like to be kept waiting and, whatever Fyfe may say, I shall have to go with him because I am under age and he is my Guardian.'

That was another matter she had lied about, she reflected, and now she would have to confess that she was very young and very inexperienced and, if the truth was known, very foolish.

'Now Fyfe too will despise me,' she thought miserably.

It was then she heard a whistle and knew at once that it was Clint looking for her.

He had a strange rather melodious way of whistling. He often whistled quietly when he moved about the Villa and, when she heard him calling for one of the other servants he whistled in a manner that was not unlike the call of a bird.

Slowly, feeling as if her legs would not carry her, Susanna stood up knowing that Clint was going to tell her that her father was waiting to see her.

She walked along the twisting path that led between the trees and back up an incline into the cultivated part of the garden.

As she expected, Clint was standing at the edge of the lawn whistling.

When he saw her, he waved his arm and, because she knew that he expected it, Susanna waved back.

Then, without waiting for her to reach him, Clint turned and walked back towards the Villa.

Somehow, although she knew that she should do so, Susanna could not move quickly.

It seemed almost as if her feet were determined to oppose her will and refuse to take her back to face what had to be faced.

Yet slowly and inevitably she crossed the lawn, passing the lilies that filled the air with their fragrance, but she did not even look at them.

She walked with her eyes staring straight ahead of her and she thought that the sunshine was dimmed and that darkness encompassed her.

She reached the verandah and now she drew in her breath, knowing that she would see her father either sitting by Fyfe's chair or standing beside it.

Then, incredibly, so that for the moment she could hardly believe it, there was no one there but Fyfe, lying back in the armchair, his legs crossed and comfortably at his ease, but alone!

So swiftly that her feet hardly seemed to touch the ground Susanna was beside him.

"Where is – Papa ? Why is he not – with you?"

Fyfe put out his hand and she laid her fingers in it.

"It's all right," he said quietly. "Your father has gone."

"Gone? But – why? What did he say? Oh – Fyfe – !"

The tears were back again in her eyes and now she knelt at his feet and put her face down against his knees.

"It's all right. I have told you it's all right. It must have been horrible for you having to wait but I sent for you as soon as I could."

"What – happened?"

It was almost impossible for Susanna to say the words, but he heard them.

"I had a long talk with your father," Fyfe replied, "and he has gone back to Florence where he will stay the night. If you want to see him, you can drive in now and talk to him. If not, he will leave first thing tomorrow morning."

Susanna raised her head from Fyfe's knees.

"I – don't – understand. What did you – say to him – how did you make him go?"

"That I am going to tell you, Susanna. But I wish you had trusted me and told me who you were."

"I did not – want anyone to – know. Did Papa – tell you why I – ran away?"

"You told me," Fyfe answered, "and your father confirmed that you were to make a brilliant Society marriage."

"I cannot marry the Duke or – any man who only wants me for my – money," Susanna said in a strangled tone.

"No, of course not," Fyfe agreed. "It is a barbarous idea and absolutely impossible for somebody like yourself."

"Did you – make Papa understand that?"

"Not exactly," Fyfe replied. "I realised that he genuinely thought that such a marriage was for your own good and he would certainly not listen to any arguments on the subject."

Susanna drew in her breath.

"That – is what I – thought. But how did he – find me?"

"I am afraid that was my fault."

"*Your* fault?"

"The reporters who were here emblazoned the story, apparently in the English newspapers as well as the American, that I was convalescing in Florence after my accident. They also said that I had been operated on in Moorfields Hospital and that I had stayed in London at 96 Curzon Street, which is a house that also belongs to me."

"I know what – happened," Susanna said quickly. "James, who is one of our footmen, must have told Papa – that I went there."

Fyfe smiled.

"That is exactly what happened. When he learned that you had visited anyone as important as Fyfe Falcon, he told your father where he had escorted you."

He gave a little laugh and added,

"Your footman had heard of me, even if you had not!"

"So Papa – followed us to Florence."

"Exactly. But he was quite surprised to find that you were earning your living as a reader."

"But is he really prepared – to let me go on doing so?" Susanna asked. "What could you have said to him to make him agree?"

"As I understood that you wanted him to go back and leave you here, I said the only thing that would make him do so."

"What – was that?"

"I said we were married!"

For a moment Susanna felt she could not have heard him aright.

Then, as she sat back on her heels, staring up at him, Fyfe said,

"I was only anticipating to your father the proposition that I was going to put in front of you once I could see again."

"Prop – propos-ition?" Susanna repeated, stuttering over the word.

He put out his hand, groping to find her, and then very gently touched the top of her head.

"Do you really think I could possibly do without you?" he asked.

"But – Fyfe – I cannot – "

Even as the words rose to her lips he sat forward in his chair and, putting his arms around her, pulled her against him.

For a moment she meant to resist, but before she could even try to do so, she was close in his arms and, as she stared at him in bewilderment, his lips came down on hers.

It was impossible to move or to think and then she knew that this was what she had longed for, yearned for and prayed for.

This was *love*, the love that she had thought never to know and the kiss she had never expected to receive.

Fyfe's arms were very strong and it flashed through Susanna's mind that he had captured her completely and she was no longer herself but a part of him.

Then the wonder of his lips swept her into the ecstasy that she had known when she had imagined herself to be Venus and been one with the stars and the fireflies.

But now it was more wonderful, more intense, Divine, yet human and she felt as if the rapture of it was so perfect that she would die from sheer happiness.

Fyfe's lips seemed to become more possessive, more insistent and more demanding, and Susanna knew that this was what she felt as if he was not only himself but also Lorenzo the Magnificent.

It was as if they had found each other across centuries of time since they had last been together.

*

Fyfe raised his head and in a voice that did not sound in the least like her own, Susanna murmured,

"I – love you! I love you – and I never thought you would – kiss me."

"I have been wanting to kiss you for a very long time," he answered. "But, my darling, I meant to wait until I could offer you a whole man not a battered, eyeless creature who has to be led about."

"Do you – really love – me?"

"I have loved you since I first heard your voice and thought that it was the most alluring and attractive sound I have ever heard in my life and, since we have been here together, I have loved you more every day."

"I love – you too," she whispered, "but I never – imagined that you – could care for me."

Even as she spoke, she remembered all too clearly why she had thought that and her whole body cried out with agony because, when he saw the truth, he would no longer love her.

'I shall have to go away before that happens,' she told herself.

Then because the thought of leaving him was like being told that she was to be executed, she pressed herself a little closer to him and felt his instant response as his lips sought hers again.

"You are so soft and sweet," he sighed, "and your mouth is exactly as I knew it would be."

"Did you – think about – kissing me?" Susanna whispered.

"I have thought of little else these last few days since my bandages were taken away," Fyfe replied. "I kept telling myself that I had to wait but, when your father told me that he intended to take you back to London with him, I just knew that I could not let you go."

"I could not – bear to think of – leaving you."

Then, as if she had only just thought of it, she asked,

"Was Papa very – angry?"

"I think he was more surprised than anything else," Fyfe replied.

"First that we should have met each other and then that I should have wanted to marry you not knowing who you were."

Susanna held her breath.

Supposing her father had said how plain she was and how unattractive? But he had apparently not done so because Fyfe went on,

"I could hardly tell him it was love at first sight when I was unable to see, but I told him that we had fallen in love with each other in a manner that made us absolutely convinced that the only sensible thing to do was to get married."

"Did Papa ask – where we were – married?"

"As a matter of fact he did not. He was too surprised that it had happened to ask many questions. He suggested, however, that all formalities regarding your fortune should be left in the hands of our Solicitors."

Before Susanna could speak he laughed.

"At least your father could not accuse me of being a fortune-hunter!"

"I think Papa must have been – impressed that – you are who – you are."

"Perhaps his surprise at our marriage was due to the fact that he had heard I was a confirmed bachelor."

Again Susanna held her breath.

She knew exactly what her father had felt – surprise that Fyfe, who was so well known and handsome, should have wanted to marry anyone as plain and unattractive as herself.

'Why did I not tell him from the very beginning?' she asked herself, but knew that it was too late now to have regrets.

Because she had a sudden terror that he might at any moment be able to see her and realise what sort of woman he had committed himself to, she whispered,

"Please kiss me – kiss me and tell me you – love me."

It was all she would have to remember, she thought, but at least it was better than nothing.

"I love you, my golden-voiced darling," Fyfe said very tenderly. "I love your voice, your sharp, fascinating little brain and, when my bandages are off, I shall love your face."

He did not wait for her answer, but his lips held hers captive and she knew as he kissed her and felt the ecstasy and the wonder of it envelop her like a shining light that any pain and agony in the future was worth this wild unearthly happiness.

'1 love – you! *I love – you*!' she cried in her heart and felt that her love joined with his and carried them both into a cloudless sky.

# CHAPTER SEVEN

"I pack ze trunks, *signorina*," Francesca said in broken English, which she wished to learn, as she arranged Susanna's hair.

"Thank you," Susanna murmured.

"Verry upsettin' if ze *Signorina* leave. What ze *Signor* do?"

Francesca received no reply, which did not surprise her as Susanna was reading.

Some books had arrived by the noon post and she was quickly turning the pages to find something that would amuse Fyfe and spark off one of their spirited arguments.

"What I am wonderin', *signorina*," Francesca continued, reverting to her warm eloquent Italian, "is what you will wear if you do travel."

Susanna caught the last words.

"Travel? Oh, in the gown I arrived in," she answered quickly and returned to her book.

"But, *signorina*, I have not yet altered that gown," Francesca exclaimed. "It is impossible, quite impossible, to do so quickly."

Then she realised that everything she said was falling on deaf ears and merely went on muttering to herself as she hurried to the wardrobe to choose a gown for Susanna to wear to go into Florence with Mr. Chambers.

Because she had so little time to read and wanted so desperately to entertain and keep Fyfe amused, almost as soon as Susanna had arrived at the Villa and found what a competent maid Francesca was, she had evolved a routine.

It gave her the only possible opportunity for what she called 'her research'.

As soon as she went to bed, she read until everything was quiet and she thought it safe to creep across the garden to the swimming pool.

When she returned, she was usually so sleepy or else caught up into an ecstasy of happiness, which she could not break, that she went straight to sleep.

Then she would wake early and lie reading until Francesca called her. When she rose from her bed, she put herself completely in the hands of the skilful dark-eyed maid.

It was Francesca who arranged her hair, helped her first into her underclothes and petticoats and then chose a gown for her from the wardrobe.

Still reading Susanna would put out one arm or raise one leg to step into her gown and, when Francesca had finished with her, without even glancing in a mirror she would go from the bedroom to the verandah where Mr. Chambers would join her at breakfast,

It would actually have not been very helpful had she looked in a mirror because as the Villa had been decorated by a man there were extremely few mirrors and what there were, were very ancient and the glass, in most of them, had become distorted and yellowed with age.

Even at home Susanna looked in a mirror as seldom as possible and she wanted, while she was at the Villa, to forget her appearance completely.

She wanted to go on thinking of herself as the Venus she pretended to be when she was in the swimming pool and because everything around her was so beautiful she could not bear to see herself fat and plain and so spoiling it all.

She read now as she walked along the passage and only when she reached the hall where Mr. Chambers was waiting for her did she put the book down on a table and take the sunshade from him that he held out for her.

"It's very hot today," he said in answer to the question in her eyes, "and you will need it if you don't wear a hat."

"I hate hats, as you know," Susanna replied, "and I love the feel of the sun on my head."

"But you must not burn yourself."

"Is Fyfe – asleep?"

She had hoped that she could have kissed him goodbye, even though they would be in Florence only for a few hours.

"Clint has put him to rest and I think he would be very angry if you disturbed him."

Susanna gave a little sigh.

It was an agony, she thought, to be away from Fyfe even for a few minutes let alone half the afternoon.

When she had gone into him this morning feeling that it was hard to believe that she had been dreaming yesterday when he said he loved her, he had pulled her into his arms and kissed her until the whole room spun around her and everything she had wanted to say was forgotten.

She could only whisper, as she had done before,

"I love – you!"

"And I love you, my darling," Fyfe said. "Last night I lay awake for a long time thinking that I am the luckiest man in the world."

"You are so wonderful – so magnificent."

He gave a little laugh.

"Am I really reaching the heights of Lorenzo? I thought that adjective applied only to him."

"That is what you are – and so much more," Susanna said passionately.

He kissed her again and then said,

"Clint has been angry with me for getting so excited about you that I did not sleep as well as I usually do."

"Oh – I am sorry! And I could not sleep either – thinking that I must have been dreaming."

"I will make you believe it is no dream unless I am dreaming too," Fyfe in his deep voice.

"You must rest," Susanna said quickly, "and you are not to get overexcited."

"I *am* over excited," he said. "How could I be anything else when I can touch you and kiss you as I have wanted to do for so long?"

His words made Susanna feel as if she were walking on clouds of glory, but she said,

"We must be sensible until you are really well, Fyfe, I could not bear that you should be ill again now when you have seemed so fit in every way."

"I promise you," he replied, "that I will try to sleep this afternoon."

Susanna felt a little stab of regret because she could not be with him, but she said softly,

"That is wise and I will not disturb you."

"You do that whenever I think of you," Fyfe said with a smile.

Because she loved him so overwhelmingly Susanna slipped her hand into his as she said,

"You must go to sleep – but please can – I stay with you – until then?"

It was as if she was a child, and he lifted her fingers to his lips before he answered her,

"I can assure you that I have no wish to be away from you even for five minutes, but because it would be difficult for me not to send for you if you are in the Villa, I want you to go into Florence with Chambers and see some of the treasures of the City."

He paused before he added,

"I feel very neglectful as a host that you have not seen San Lorenzo, San Marco, Giotto's Campanile, the Palazzo Vecchio or the Bargello."

Susanna gave a cry.

"Stop! *Stop*! If I see all those, I shall be away from you for weeks!"

"I was only teasing, but you must see Michaelangelo's *David* and Cellini's *Terseus* so that you can tell me if you find them more attractive than Lorenzo and, of course, me!"

"You know the answer to that already," Susanna replied.

"And while you are there you had better have just one quick look at Botticelli's *Venus* and Lippi's *Madonna* before I am in a position to tell you which you resemble."

Susanna stiffened.

"Do you – know when the doctors are – going to take off – your bandages?"

It was difficult to say the words and they came hesitatingly from her lips.

To her relief Fyfe shrugged his shoulders.

"I told Chambers to find out when they intend to do so," he replied. "He thinks it might be in several days or perhaps another week."

Susanna felt the relief sweep over her.

She had not to leave him just yet.

She could still see him and talk to him, he would kiss her and she could live for a little longer in the special Heaven that seemed to envelop them both with a blinding light.

Because she could not help herself, she moved a little nearer to him asking,

"Tell me exactly how – soon I can come back from – Florence and be with you again."

"Shall we say five o'clock?" he answered.

"So long?" Susanna exclaimed.

"I find it very difficult to argue with Clint when he is bullying me into taking care of myself," Fyfe smiled. "He always has very convincing arguments as to why I should do what he wants. Today it is because I must be well for you."

"In that case," Susanna said in a small voice, "Clint is – right. Of course I love you too much to do anything – to make you ill."

She spoke as if she was convincing herself, knowing despairingly that once Fyfe was really well she would never see him again.

'When he can see,' she thought, 'I will still be in his mind as he imagined me, like Simonette Vespucci or Lucretia Buti and he will never, never know what Susanna Laven was like in reality.'

"Why are you thinking sad thoughts when we are so happy?" Fyfe asked.

She started a little guiltily.

"How do you know – they are sad?"

"I am using my *Third Eye* or shall I say I always use it where you are concerned?"

"Of course I am not sad," Susanna said in a positive voice. "How could I be, when I am – close to you and you have said you – love me?"

She looked up at him pleadingly as she added,

"You do really love me – more than you have – loved anyone else?"

"I know now that I have never loved anyone else," Fyfe affirmed. "All the women I have known in the past have disappointed me in one way or another. I think really it was because they pleased my eyes, but my mind found them wanting in so many different ways."

His lips curved in the smile she loved before he added,

"I know you are waiting for me to say that those perceptions of mine, which have matured under your guidance, tell me that you are everything I want and need in my life. In fact you are the other half of me."

Because she was so moved Susanna felt the tears gather in her eyes, but she forced herself to say lightly,

"I should never – aspire to being the other half of *Fyfe the Magnificent*, but I am content – very content to be a – shadow of your heart."

"Not the shadow," he replied, "but in my heart and part of my heart. Indeed I am not certain that you are not the whole heart itself."

As she spoke, he drew her back into his arms and kissed her again.

Then when her breath came quickly from between her lips and she felt her whole body respond to him, she hid her face against his shoulder and his hand touched her hair.

"It feels like silk," he murmured. "Florentine silk which is made here and which we will buy together when I can choose the colour for you that will suit you best."

Susanna found it impossible to answer him and he went on,

"Tell me how long your hair is. I can feel from the amount that is piled so neatly on your small head that it is full and long and covers your shoulders like a soft cloud."

"You are – making me – shy."

"I shall like you shy," he answered, "when I can see the colour rise in your cheeks."

Every word he spoke made Susanna remember in anguish that she had so little time left.

How would he ever think her dull hair beautiful? Although in fact it was quite long, it had always looked lank and rather rat-tailed and not in the least like the cloud of glory he imagined it to be.

"Once I can see again," Fyfe was saying, "I shall only want to look at you, my precious one, but there are so many things we can do together. I am glad in some ways that you have seen so little of Florence. I so want to show you my own favourite statues and pictures."

He pressed his lips for a moment against her forehead.

"Any women I have ever taken to see them in the past have always been so extraordinarily ignorant about art that it has irritated me. I know that is something I will never feel with you."

Susanna made a little murmur and he went on,

"In Florence, Paris, London and New York there are a million things for us to see and enjoy. I feel because I love you that the whole world is there for us to discover, but without you it would be just as it is to me now, nothing but darkness."

"You must – not say – that," Susanna protested.

"It is true," he said. "You have brought a light into my darkness since the first moment in London when you read to me in that miraculous voice of yours. If you should go away, I will become blind again to everything you have taught me to see."

"No, *no*!" Susanna cried. "You must not say that. You are you! Magnificent, self-sufficient, and brilliant. You do not – need me."

"It is going to take me a lifetime to tell you how much I need you and want you."

Then he kissed her again and she could think of nothing but him and the love she felt for him.

It had been hard to leave Fyfe at luncheontime, but he had said when she had first known him,

"I am not going to let anybody see me making a fool of myself while I am fed like a child. If I need a drink, you will leave the room."

He had spoken harshly, almost roughly, for in those days he was still fighting against his blindness and loathing his disability.

Susanna had half-hoped when the bandages were removed from his mouth that she could stay with him at mealtimes, but he had always sent her away, saying,

"I still have to have my food cut up for me. I still upset things and eat untidily and I prefer to do so in private."

Susanna could understand his feelings, for she had learnt that he was a very fastidious person.

"Always tidy, always neat about his person," Clint had said to her one day. "That's why you'll understand, miss, the relief I felt when I saw his face wasn't scarred. He couldn't bear to look ugly and that was one of the things I was real afraid of."

What Clint had said had been another spur to Susanna's determination that he must never see her.

Of course, being so handsome himself and being surrounded all his life with such beautiful things, he would want the woman he loved to be beautiful too.

She had made her plans very carefully.

She would have everything packed so that when the doctors arrived to take off the bandages, she would tell the servants that she had received a cable and must leave for London immediately.

They would bring the carriage to the door, her luggage would be placed inside and she would just wait for the doctors to come from Fyfe's room so that she would know the truth.

If he could see, she would leave quickly before he had time to ask for her.

On the other hand if the worst happened and he was blind, he would need her and it would not matter in the least what she looked like.

It all seemed so simple, but she knew that it was going to crucify her to go away and yet at the same time she had no alternative.

How could she stay, she asked herself, and see the disappointment in Fyfe's eyes gradually turn to the contempt and disdain with that mother had always regarded her with.

And what was more his feelings might become those of hatred simply because she had lied to him and imposed on his credulity.

The fact that while Fyfe rested she and Mr. Chambers were going into Florence gave her an excuse to ask him for some money.

"I am afraid you were right and I spent rather a lot on Fyfe's birthday present," she said. "I should be very grateful if you could let me have my wages, even though I think they are not due for another day or so."

"Of course you can have them," Mr. Chambers replied, "and if you would like to borrow on the future I will advance you as much as you wish."

Susanna wanted to say that he must not pay her for what she would be unable to earn, but she replied,

"I shall be very content with a month's salary. It would be a mistake I think to carry too much money around with me."

"Yes, of course," he agreed.

Now as she stepped into the carriage he handed her an envelope, which she knew contained enough at any rate for her fare to England or for her to stay at an inexpensive hotel somewhere in Italy.

She had not really decided whether having lost Fyfe she would go home or whether she would seek employment abroad.

She was quite certain that it would not be difficult because of her proficiency in languages and yet the idea of being alone and lonely was now much more frightening than it had been when she had first decided to run away.

It was knowing Fyfe and loving him which had made the future seem, as he would have put it, completely and absolutely dark because he was not there.

'What am I to do?' Susanna asked herself a thousand times.

But she could find no answer to her question and she told herself that it was because for the moment she could think only of Fyfe and the precious glorious moments when she could be with him.

"Where are we going first?" she asked Mr. Chambers.

"Wherever you would like," he answered. "I have strict instructions from Fyfe to keep you away from the Villa until five o'clock. Otherwise he says, he will break all Clint's regulations and demand your attendance on him."

Susanna gave a little sigh and Mr. Chambers went on,

"I have never known Fyfe so happy or so in love."

"There must have been – many women in his life," Susanna said in a low voice.

"I will not insult your intelligence by answering that untruthfully," Mr. Chambers replied. "Women have pursued him ever since he was a very young man."

"I expected – that."

"It was understandable. He was not only handsome and extremely clever but the only child of one of the richest men in America."

"I had no idea he is as rich as – that."

"Old Mr. Falcon, who was as clever as his son, invested in Railroads in their infancy and also bought the land that they were likely to travel over."

"While Fyfe likes motor cars."

"He likes anything that is progressive, moves quickly and keeps his mind stimulated and active, as you do."

"You cannot expect me to – compete with the Falcon car."

"That is exactly what you have done," Mr. Chambers smiled, "and that is why I am so grateful to you. You have given him something that no one else has been able to do before."

Susanna looked at him enquiringly and he finished,

"And the knowledge that intellectually he can survive any physical disability, even blindness."

"I think he would have found that out – eventually on his – own."

"I doubt it," Mr. Chambers said. "If you had seen the state he was in when we crossed the Atlantic, you would have known that he would have preferred to die rather than face the knowledge that he must spend the rest of his life in darkness."

"That must not – happen!" Susanna said quickly.

"I pray that our optimism will be well founded, but, if disastrously the worst happens, then I believe with your help he will find that there are quite a number of useful things he can do in the world even without the use of his eyes."

"I have thought of that," Susanna said. "He could, of course, advise and – attend the meetings of his Company."

"We have been thinking along the same lines," Mr. Chambers nodded, "but I am sure in my heart, partly because he has always been lucky and also because you have given him hope and faith in himself. that there is now more than a fifty-fifty chance that he will come through it all triumphantly."

"I feel that too," Susanna answered. "I feel it so strongly – that I know in my heart he will see as – well as I do."

She spoke prophetically and she knew that her *Third Eye* could not be mistaken where Fyfe was concerned.

Despite the fact that she was longing to go back to the Villa, Susanna could not help being thrilled by Michelangelo's statue of David.

She was also entranced by the Michelangelo sculptures that surrounded the magnificent tomb built for Lorenzo.

It was impossible to think even for a moment of Lorenzo without longing for Fyfe and finding that his personality seemed to be superimposed upon everything she looked at.

It was four o'clock when Mr. Chambers insisted, because Fyfe had told him to do so, that they should go to the Uffizi Gallery.

He could not understand that Susanna had no wish to look at the exquisite face of Botticelli's *Venus* or Lippi's *Madonna and the Angels*.

But because she knew that Mr. Chambers would not understand her refusal to do what she was asked, she stood in front of the *Birth of Venus* looking despairingly at the soft oval of Simonetta's face, her blue eyes and her red gold hair falling over her white shoulders.

She thought as she turned away that she would hate the idea of Venus, any Venus, for the rest of her life.

"Now we can go home," Mr Chambers said with a smile. "Are you tired?"

"Not in the least," Susanna answered.

The idea of seeing Fyfe again had brought the sparkle to her eyes, her heart was beating more quickly and little thrills of excitement were running through her because in a very short while she would be close to him and perhaps in his arms.

'I want him to kiss me,' she thought. 'I want it more than I have ever wanted anything in my whole life or will ever want anything again.'

She felt that the horses were climbing the hill with infuriating slowness, but at last they reached the outside of the Villa and she could not wait for the footmen to jump down from the box and open the door of the carriage but did it herself.

Then she ran up the steps.

Clint was waiting in the hall.

"Is the Master awake?" Susanna asked him breathlessly.

"He's anxious to see you, miss," Clint answered. "But I expect you'd like to tidy yourself up first. There's a cool drink waitin' for you in your bedroom. It must have been like a furnace in the City."

"It was," Susanna answered.

She would have liked to go to Fyfe straight away.

Then she thought perhaps if he kissed her, her cheeks would be hot and he would be aware that her hair had been blown a little from the breeze that came from the Arno.

She went into her bedroom and found Francesca there.

"It must have been very hot in the City, *signorina*," she said, echoing Clint. "I've a cool gown ready for you to change into and there's water ready for you in the basin."

Impatiently, because she was grudging every second she could not be with Fyfe, Susanna washed and let Francesca change her gown.

The maid brushed her hair into place and then running because she was in such a hurry Susanna crossed the room and sped down the passage towards Fyfe's bedroom.

Clint was waiting at the door to open it for her and she went in, her eyes alight and a smile on her lips.

Then she checked herself suddenly to find not, as she expected, that Fyfe was alone, but there were several other people in the room with him.

She looked at them in astonishment, wondering who they were and why they were strangely dressed.

Then Fyfe, who was standing in the centre of the room only a little way from her, held out his hand.

"Come here, Susanna."

She obeyed him and he took her hand in his and held it very closely.

"Because, my darling," he said, "1 regret having had to lie to your father and because I want more than I can tell you that you should belong to me, I have asked the Chaplain of the American Embassy to marry us, which he has consented to do."

Susanna gave a gasp and now she realised that an elderly man in the room was dressed in a cassock and that the two young men with him also wore cassocks but of a different colour.

"It will only be a short Service, Miss Laven," the Chaplain said. "And you are doubtless aware that by American law it is perfectly legal for me to marry you here in the Villa."

Susanna felt as if her voice had died in her throat.

She must stop this.

She could not marry Fyfe.

She must tell him so and why.

Then, as he drew her forward towards the Chaplain, she knew that she could not speak to him about herself in front of strangers.

How could she explain, how could she tell him that she had lied, that she was not beautiful? How could she destroy the wonder and splendour of their love by confessing to her own selfish personal deceit?

'I cannot marry him! I cannot for his sake,' Susanna cried in her mind.

But her heart told her that she could not hurt him and could not embarrass and shame him in front of a Chaplain from his country's Embassy.

As she waited, trying frantically to think what she should do, the Chaplain opened his Prayer Book and began the Marriage Service.

It was very short and, when Fyfe had taken his vows in a deep sincere voice that seemed to vibrate through Susanna, she heard almost as if it was the voice of a stranger, her own faltering responses.

As if he understood some of the tumult within her, Fyfe held her hand tightly all the time they were being married.

The strength of his fingers seemed in some strange way to sweep away everything else except for their love.

'It is because I love him that I should try to save him from himself,' she tried to tell herself.

Instead she could only think that her body seemed to throb over and over again with three words,

"I love you – I love you – "

One of the Servers handed Fyfe a ring and the Chaplain blessed it before it was placed on her finger.

She knew, as she helped Fyfe by putting her finger in exactly the right place, that she should not be doing this, that it was wrong and when he knew the truth he might throw her violently out of his house and out of his life because she had deceived him.

And yet insidiously, beneath everything else, was the incredible joy in knowing that she was now Fyfe's wife and because of it she could not be forced into marrying anybody else.

The Service came to an end. They knelt, the Chaplain blessed them and, as they rose from their knees, Fyfe raised Susanna's hand to his lips.

"I love you, my darling!" he whispered very softly so that only she could hear.

After that it seemed too bewildering for her to realise what was really happening.

Clint came into the room with glasses of champagne, while Mr. Chambers joined them, as did all the servants in the Villa, congratulating them in their warm Italian, as happy, Susanna thought, as if they had been married themselves.

It was only when the Chaplain said 'goodbye' and Mr. Chambers went with him to the door while the servants vanished into their own quarters, that Susanna found herself alone with her husband.

They were standing side by side as they said 'goodbye' and 'thank you' to the Chaplain and, as Fyfe heard the door close, he turned to put his arms round her.

For a moment she thought that she ought to struggle against him and make him listen to her, to tell him that she should have refused to marry him, but had been unable to do so.

Then it was too late.

He was kissing her and there was nothing in the world but him —

It seemed to Susanna that they had only been together for a few seconds although it must have been very much longer, before Clint came to tell them that dinner would be ready in half an hour.

"Is it so late?" she exclaimed.

"Time for the Master to go to bed, ma'am," Clint replied.

"To bed?" Susanna echoed in surprise, "but I thought —
"

"He's still tired, ma'am," Clint said, before Fyfe could speak, "and all this excitement, as you well know, is bad for him."

He saw the disappointment in Susanna's face and added,

"There's tomorrow, if you'll excuse my sayin' so, ma'am, and many years ahead for you to talk it over, but I'm not havin' the Master gettin' over-tired or over-excited and that's what he is at this moment."

"Give us five minutes to say 'goodnight'," Fyfe ordered, "and then I will let you put me to bed as you want to, Clint."

"Very good, sir."

Clint went from the room and Fyfe pulled Susanna into his arms.

"I love you!" he beamed, "and, as Clint says, we have many years when I can tell you so and make you believe it."

"Has it – really been – too much for you?" she asked anxiously. "How could I have guessed you were – planning anything so – extraordinary when you sent me into Florence?"

"I never thought I could keep such a monumental secret from you," Fyfe said. "I have a feeling that your *Third Eye* has broken down and needs repairing!"

"If I had a thousand eyes, I should never have thought that you would do anything so wonderful and yet so – outrageous as marrying me without even – asking me if I would be your – wife."

"Are you sorry?"

"No, no. I could – never be sorry," Susanna answered, "not as long as you – love me and will go on – loving me."

She thought as she spoke that was unlikely, but for the moment the nearness of him and the fact that his lips were seeking hers made it impossible to say or think of anything but that it was a wonder beyond wonders to be his wife.

He kissed her until Clint knocked on the door.

And then he said,

"When you go to bed, my precious darling, dream of me as I shall dream of you and tomorrow we will plan our honeymoon."

It was impossible for the moment to answer him, for her voice was lost in the rapture that his kisses had aroused in her.

They moved apart and Fyfe called out, 'come in' and, as Clint entered the room, Susanna left.

She wanted to be alone, she wanted to think, but Francesca was waiting for her and automatically she changed again into an evening gown to dine with Mr. Chambers.

She noticed when she went into the dining room where they ate their evening meal that the table was decorated with white flowers.

With a little throb of her heart she thought that it should be Fyfe sitting at the head of the table and Fyfe she should be dining with on her Wedding night.

Because she was very fond of Mr. Chambers and she did not wish him to know what she was thinking, they talked about Falcon Motors and Fyfe's mother, who had died when he had been quite young.

Then he told her of how Fyfe had never really had a home although he owned houses in many parts of the world.

"That is what I feel you will give him," Mr. Chambers said. "A home where he will have roots and where he will settle down."

Susanna knew without his saying so that Fyfe would want a family and that was what he himself had always lacked in being an only child.

They talked until Susanna thought that perhaps Mr. Chambers was becoming tired and she suggested that they should leave the dining room.

He seemed quite ready to say 'goodnight' to her and she went to her room where Francesca undressed her as she had always done and brushed her hair while she read.

When she finally climbed into bed, she went on reading for a little while and then put down her book to think about Fyfe.

For the first time she noticed that her trunks, which had been packed and which stood in an alcove in her room, had been taken away.

'The servants would not expect me to leave now,' she told herself, 'but that is what I ought to do.'

Yet how was it possible to leave now that she was married to Fyfe?

For him to lose a wife would be very different from losing a reader.

'What shall I do? *What shall I do*?' she asked the night air.

The question turned into a prayer, but it seemed as if there was no answer.

Automatically, because she had done so every night, she rose when everything was quiet to go to the swimming pool.

When she pulled back the curtains, which Francesca had drawn over the windows, she found that it was a moonlit night, as it had been on the first time that she had found her way through the garden.

Everything was illuminated with a radiance that was so lovely, so ethereal and mystic that it seemed appropriate for her Wedding night – except that she was alone.

Susanna walked out through the window in her bare feet, wearing only the thin nightgown that she had gone to bed in.

Before she left her room she did what she had always done and piled her hair on top of her head, pinning it securely so that it would not get wet.

Then she moved over the grass feeling that it still warm from the heat of the sun.

There was the fragrance of the flowers, especially the lilies, and Susanna felt that they enveloped her tonight more than they had ever done before, simply because every nerve in her body was throbbing with the awareness of her love.

There seemed to be more stars in the sky than ever and more fireflies in the air and they flew before her until she reached the swimming pool.

She thought as they flashed above the water that they were like the golden sparkle of champagne.

'If only Fyfe was with me,' she mused with a little sigh.

Then she told herself that if he was, he would not look at her with love, but perhaps with horror.

She took off her nightgown and threw it on the ground, and walked slowly down into the pool, pretending, as she always did, to be the Venus whose pictured face she had looked at only a few hours ago.

Yet tonight, instead she knew that she was only herself. Susanna, immortalised not by the brush of a Master painter but by the love that filled her heart to the exclusion of all else.

She walked deeper and deeper and then struck out, swimming amongst the fireflies as she had done before.

Tonight her eyes were almost blinded by the reflection of the moonlight on the water and after a while she closed them and swam in a haze of happiness still feeling Fyfe's kisses on her lips.

She must have gone up and down the pool nearly a dozen times before she stopped at the shallow end and stood up with the water just below her waist.

As she did so, she looked up at the moon and remembered how on the first night she had prayed to the Heavens to give her love.

'I am grateful, so very very grateful,' she told the stars.

She raised her arms as she had done before not in supplication but in gratitude.

Then as she did so with her head thrown back, quite suddenly, she was not alone!

Someone was standing in the water beside her and, as she gave a little gasp, she saw by the light of the moon that it was Fyfe!

For a moment she thought that she must be imagining him for there was no bandage round his head and he was looking straight at her.

Then, as she turned as it seemed to stone, his arms came towards her and she knew that he was real, very real, as he pulled her close to him.

"My sweet, my darling," he said. "My own Venus whom I have longed to see like this."

She gave a cry of horror and hid her face against his shoulder.

"Don't – look at me! Please – don't look at me!"

"Why not, when I have been looking at you for some time. And you are the most beautiful woman I have ever seen."

"You – can see? You can – really – *see*?"

"I can see, but I shall have to wear dark glasses during the day. That is why, my darling, I wanted to see you tonight in the light of the moon."

"B-but you – cannot see me – clearly?" Susanna insisted.

"I can see very clearly," Fyfe answered, "and I cannot allow you to hide from me as now at least I have eyes to see as well as ears to hear."

He put his fingers under her chin as he spoke and turned her face up to his.

'Now he will – see what I am really like,' she thought in an agony and closed her eyes so that she would not see the expression on his face change.

She felt that he looked at her for a long time, but it must have been only for a few seconds before he said,

"You are just as your voice told me you would look!"

"I-I think you must – still be – blind," she faltered.

"Open your eyes and look at me, my precious."

Trembling against him she obeyed him and saw his eyes just as she had imagined, gazing deep into hers as if they searched her very soul.

"I – am – sorry – very sorry," she whispered, "I did not – mean to lie to you – but I wanted to pretend I was – beautiful – because you thought I was."

"You *are* beautiful!" he stated positively.

Then, as if he could not help himself, he drew her closer still and his lips found hers.

His kiss swept away for the moment every thought but love and Susanna could feel the sensations he aroused in her moving like a flame through her breasts and into her lips.

Still holding her captive with his mouth, Fyfe reached up and pulled away the hairpins so that her hair fell over her shoulders.

Then he raised his head and, with his arm round Susanna, he drew her out of the water.

~183~

They walked up the steps side by side, but she could not even feel shy that they were both naked, but only bewildered because he had looked at her and not found her ugly.

He drew her across the grass and then pulled her down onto what she realised was a heap of large, comfortable silk cushions which were screened on three sides by cypress trees.

Susanna looked up and saw Fyfe's head silhouetted against the stars.

The moonlight illuminated them both and below them the fireflies still danced over the silver pool.

Then Fyfe lay beside her and drew her into his arms.

"I have a great deal of explaining to do, my precious one," he said. "First you must forgive me for sending you away when the doctors came this afternoon to remove my bandages."

"Th-this – afternoon!"

"I not only wanted to learn the truth about myself, but I was terrified, yes, *terrified* that you intended to run away and leave me."

She turned her face against his shoulder.

"How – did you – know that?"

"First of all I used my *Third Eye* and I knew that there was something wrong, although you would not tell me what it was. Then, I admit, I was rather helped by the fact that Francesca told Clint that you had asked for your trunks to be packed."

"I – did not – want you to – see me," Susanna whispered.

"I already sensed that there was some mystery about your appearance. You see, my darling one, your voice is very expressive and because it means so much to me I now know every inflection in it and every secret you try to keep from me."

He gave a little laugh as he pulled her even closer.

"Let me assure you it will be very difficult for you ever to deceive me in the future, in fact I am quite certain that you would be unable to do so."

"I would not – wish to – deceive you," Susanna murmured "but you – ought to have married somebody – beautiful like all the – beautiful women you have around you."

"I *have* married somebody beautiful!"

He knew without her answering that she did not believe him and after a moment he asked,

"When did you last look in your mirror?"

"I never look in one if I can possibly – avoid it," Susanna answered violently. "I know only – too well what I will – see."

"That is where I think you are mistaken because from what everyone has told me you have altered a great deal since you have been here with me."

"How can you – know that – and what do you – mean?"

"I gather from what I have been told that when you came to Florence you were rather fat."

"Very fat!" Susanna muttered.

"It's a pity you did not weigh yourself, my darling, when you arrived, so that I could make you do so now and see the difference."

Susanna raised her head from his shoulder to look down at her body. It had never struck her to look before, because when she had swum on all the other nights she had been thinking that she was not herself but Venus.

Now she could see that certainly her breasts were very much smaller than they had been, her waist seemed to be very slim, and her stomach was completely flat.

"Have I – really altered?" she asked incredulously.

"Francesca, who has had to take in your dresses almost every day, told me that your hair has a buoyancy about it that it never had before and there are golden lights in it from the sun."

Susanna drew in her breath before she whispered,

"And – my – face?"

Fyfe raised himself on his elbow so that he could look down at her.

"Shall I tell you about it, my sweet? It is rather thin, pointing down to a small chin, but let me start at the top."

He kissed her forehead.

"Your forehead is as you wanted it to be, like the Madonna in the Lippi picture, but your eyes are very much larger than Simonetta's. They seem to fill your little face and I adore the winged eyebrows above them."

He outlined them with his finger as he spoke. Then he ran it down her small straight nose.

"Perhaps that was somewhat lost when you were fat," he commented, "but now it is perfectly proportioned and your mouth is exactly as it should be, an invitation for my kisses."

He bent his head, but Susanna put up her hands to hold him back.

"Are you – are you telling me the – truth – the real *truth*?"

"I swear before God that you are beautiful, very beautiful, my darling one, and because you have made me intelligent about other things besides motor cars I think I know exactly what has happened."

"Tell – me! *Tell me!*"

"Well, first of all from the moment you arrived here you went on the same diet as Chambers, no sugar at all, so your fat must have melted away day by day."

He smiled as he added,

"Sugar is poison to some people."

As he spoke, Susanna thought guiltily of all the chocolates and sweets she had consumed in the past whenever her mother had made her feel inferior and unloved.

Of course she had stuffed herself with sweets that made her fat and she remembered too the enormous meals that she had eaten at home.

Three or four different dishes for breakfast and she had gobbled up the huge stodgy puddings that had been served in the schoolroom at luncheontime.

Roly-poly puddings full of sultanas and treacle sauce and endless sponges covered with strawberry jam.

It was not surprising that she had been fat, because with her stomach full, she had not felt so miserable nor so insignificant.

"And not only did you lose weight that way," Fyfe was saying, "but every night when you swam up and down the swimming pool you were exercising all the right muscles to make your body as perfect as it is now."

His hand touched her breast as he spoke and outlined her hip and she felt herself quiver at the thrill of it, but she could not help asking,

"Did you – know I swam – every night?"

"Of course I knew," he answered. "Nothing is ever hidden or secret when you live in Italy. The man who looks after the swimming pool knew that it had been used and Clint, who sleeps with one eye open, was aware that you crept through the garden when you thought that everybody was asleep. I used to listen to you passing my window and longed to join you."

He smiled as he added very tenderly,

"That is why I knew this was where I should find you tonight to tell you my secrets, so that we should no longer hide anything from each other."

He moved his lips against the softness of her cheek as he went on,

"You were a voice in the dark, my sweet darling, a sweet golden voice but now I can see you and I love what I see!"

"You mean – you really mean that I am not – ugly – and you are not – disgusted by me?"

"I can answer the last part of that question very easily," Fyfe replied with a deep note in his voice. "But I promise you, my precious heart, that I am telling you the truth when I say that you are very lovely and I am only afraid that a great number of other men will want to tell you the same. You are beautiful because love is beautiful and as our love grows you will be more beautiful still."

"Do you think I would ever want to listen to – anybody but you?" Susanna asked. "Oh, Fyfe, if you really think me pretty – enough for you – then I need not leave you."

"I have no intention of letting you leave me," he replied. "I am very angry with you for even thinking of doing so. How do you think I could live without you? And how could you be so cruel and so wicked as to want to leave me in darkness again?"

"Oh my darling, I have no wish to – do so," Susanna cried. "I love and adore you! You are wonderful – magnificent – and you fill my whole – world. I just cannot believe I am – worthy of you."

"You are everything I ever wanted in a woman and thought never to find," Fyfe said. "Our whole life together, my precious one, will be one of such beauty that never again will you see ugliness anywhere, especially in your adorable, perfect little face."

His lips found hers as he spoke and now, because his words had moved her into an ecstasy that surpassed anything she had ever known, Susanna's arms went round him as he held her close and closer still.

She knew, as she felt his heart beating against hers, the strength and warmth of his body, that they were one, not only with themselves but with the wonder of the stars, the beauty of the garden and the fragrance of the lilies.

"You are mine!" Fyfe cried and his voice was deep with passion. "Mine now and for ever and I will never let you go."

Then they were no longer human, but Divine and a part of God, who is perfect beauty and shines as a dazzling light to lead mankind through the darkness to love.

# OTHER BOOKS IN THIS SERIES

The Barbara Cartland Eternal Collection is the unique opportunity to collect all five hundred of the timeless beautiful romantic novels written by the world's most celebrated and enduring romantic author.

Named the Eternal Collection because Barbara's inspiring stories of pure love, just the same as love itself, the books will be published on the internet at the rate of four titles per month until all five hundred are available.

The Eternal Collection, classic pure romance available worldwide for all time.